GW01402948

Golden Melodies

Braided Realms, Volume 1

Morgan Sterling

Published by Morgan Sterling, 2024.

GOLDEN MELODIES

First edition. November 27, 2024.

Copyright © 2024 Morgan Sterling.

ISBN: 979-8227057297

Written by Morgan Sterling.

Prelude

ELARA SENSED THE FAMILIAR feeling of an invisible hand pulling her back flush against Lorien's body. Instinctually, the Fae put a protective arm around her waist. His muscles tensed, his jaw clenched, but he said nothing. His eyes were focused on the several skirmishes that had broken out around a festive event just a short time ago.

A large man she recognized as a welder from the village threw a useless blow at a thin, wiry faerie that stood at least a foot taller. The faerie gracefully flew back, avoiding the blow, then with incredible speed moved forward, picking up the man, and flew straight up several feet before dropping him. Elara heard bones crack.

Another fae, with an amused look on its face, was wrapping three villagers up in vines using magic.

They were there to rescue Elara, but it was they who needed rescuing. In what world did they think showing up with pitchforks and righteous indignation would beat Fairies? Stronger, faster, and magical.

But here they were, ignorant and angry. Elara was ashamed, angry, and scared. Lorien must have sensed it. He tightened his grip, and she turned and buried her face into his chest with a sob.

"Get your filthy hands off my daughter," Hector yelled, again attempting to pull his Elara away. However, the ancient spell that had bound Elara to Lorien would not be released. Even if Lorien had released his grip on her waist, the enchantment wouldn't allow her more than a few inches from Lorien, if any, space at all.

And the truth is, whispering in the back of her mind was that she didn't want to be separated. She didn't want Lorien to let go.

"Enough." Lorien's voice was low, edged with a quiet anger that sent a shiver down Elara's spine. "I will not allow you to be so rough with Elara again. She is not a child to be manhandled at your whim."

"You dare presume to tell me how to treat my own daughter?" He spun to face the other villagers, his arm sweeping out in a grand gesture. "Are we to stand idly by while these creatures bewitch our children, our loved ones? I say we take back what is ours!"

When the violence erupted anew, Elara feared that those she loved and those she realized she was growing to love might never come to accept one another. She thought back to how it all started, realizing that if it wasn't for the spell, she might have never understood what ignorance had blinded her too.

Chapter 1

EYES CLOSED, SWAYING to the music all her own, Elara could almost feel him behind her, molded right to her body and swaying along. She never saw his face when she daydreamed, but she'd been increasingly daydreaming about him. Making music with her and touching her body and soul.

Sunlight streamed through the kitchen window, casting a warm glow on Elara's face as she hummed a new melody, her fingers tapping out the rhythm on the worn wooden table. It was so close to real that she could almost touch her imaginary companion, warm against her, humming a beautiful sound to match her own. Lost in the music swirling in her mind, she hardly noticed her father enter the room, his heavy footsteps breaking her concentration.

"Elara, love," Hector said, his voice a mix of affection and exasperation. "I need you to run some errands in town today. And while you're at it, gather some herbs from the edge of the forest? I'm planning a special dinner tonight."

Elara's hazel eyes widened, her curly dark hair bouncing as she turned to face her father. Her face reddened as if she'd be caught like her imagination was real. But there was no one there for her father to catch. So she recovered and stammered. "But Papa, I was just about to perfect this new song for the festival! Can't the errands wait? This melody could be my big break."

She began to hum the tune again, her body swaying to the beat. The song was almost there, just on the tip of her tongue, waiting to be unleashed. If only she had a little more time...

Hector sighed, his weathered face softening. "Elara, I know your music means the world to you, but we all have responsibilities. The errands need to be done today."

Just then, Dante sauntered into the kitchen, his mischievous grin lighting up the room. "Hey now, no need to dampen our little songbird's spirits! Why not let her do both, Pop? You know how dedicated she is to her craft."

Elara smiled gratefully at her brother. Leave it to Dante to always have her back. He was a great brother.

Dante draped an arm around Hector's shoulders, his voice smooth as honey. "Come on, Dad. Think about it. If Elara nails this song, it could be her ticket to joining the royal court as a musician. Isn't that what Mom would have wanted? For her to chase her dreams?"

Elara's heart clenched at the mention of their mother. Her mom had died when she was small; she barely remembered her, but the void the woman left was big. It had been years since her passing, but the pain was still fresh for the family. She understood her father's protectiveness stemmed from the tragic loss, but sometimes, it felt like a cage, holding her back from her true calling.

Hector's eyes misted over. Absentminded his hand reached for the locket around his neck. Inside was a picture of their mother, forever frozen in time. After a long moment, he nodded slowly.

"Alright, alright. You two always did have a way with words." He turned to Elara, his gaze intense. "You can do both tasks today. But promise me you'll be careful love. And don't go too far into the forest, you hear? Just stick to the outskirts."

Elara leaped from her chair, engulfing her father in a tight hug. "Thank you, Papa! I promise I'll be careful. And I'll find the perfect herbs for your special dinner tonight."

As she gathered her things to head out, Elara couldn't shake the sense that today would be different. The song in her heart grew louder, urging her towards something new and exciting. With a skip in her step and a melody on her lips, she set off to explore the wonders of Willowmere, unaware of the adventure that awaited her in the mystical forest beyond.

Elara stepped out into the bustling streets of Willowmere, her senses immediately awakened by the village's vibrant sights, sounds, and smells. The sun cast a warm glow over the quaint cobblestone paths, and the air was filled with friendly neighbors' chatter and birds' distant chirping.

As she made her way through the village, Elara couldn't help but hum the tune of her new song, her fingers tapping the rhythm against her thigh. She waved to the baker, who was setting out freshly baked loaves of bread, their aroma wafting through the air and mingling with the sweet scent of blooming flowers.

"Morning, Elara!" the baker called out, his round face splitting into a wide grin. "Off to run errands for your father again?"

Elara nodded, returning his smile with one of her own. "You know it, Mr. Jameson. But I'm also gathering inspiration for my new song. The festival is just around the corner, and I want it to be perfect."

The baker chuckled, his eyes crinkling at the corners. "With a voice like yours, my dear, I have no doubt it will be. Here, take a roll for the road." He tossed her a small, golden-brown bun, which she caught with a grateful smile.

As Elara continued, she couldn't help but experience a sense of belonging wash over her. This was her home, her community, and the people here were like an extended family. She greeted the seamstress, hanging colorful fabrics outside her shop, and the blacksmith, who was already hard at work at his forge.

But even as she basked in the warmth of Willowmere, Elara's thoughts drifted to the forest just beyond the village borders. It called to her, its secrets whispering to her soul. She knew her father's warnings came from a place of love and fear, but a part of her longed to explore those ancient woods, to uncover the magic that lay hidden within. Or maybe she just wanted to prove to herself that she could go back into those woods and nothing bad would happen.

"One day," she whispered, her eyes fixed on the distant treeline. "One day, I'll discover what lies beyond."

As Elara made her way through the bustling streets of Willowmere, her mind wandered to the song she'd been working on. The melody was there, the lyrics were falling into place, but something was missing. It was like a puzzle with a piece that remained just out of reach.

She hummed gently, trying different variations, but nothing seemed to fit. *What is it?* she thought, her brow furrowed in concentration. *What's the sound I need to make this song complete?*

Deep down, Elara knew her music was more than a hobby. It was a calling, a passion that burned within her. She dreamed of performing for the royal court, of sharing her songs with the world. But every time she thought of leaving Willowmere, guilt would grip her heart.

I can't leave Dad, she told herself, not for the first time. *Not after everything he's been through. He needs me.*

But even as she thought it, a small voice in her mind whispered, *But what about what you need, Elara? What about your dreams?*

She shook her head as if to dispel the thought. Her father had already lost so much. She couldn't bear the thought of causing him more pain. And yet, the longing in her heart remained as constant as the song that played in her head.

Maybe one day, she thought wistfully. *Maybe when Dad's doing better, he doesn't need me as much. Maybe then I can chase my dreams.*

For now, though, she had errands and a song to finish. And so, with a determination set on her shoulders, Elara made her way through the village, her mind split between the present and the future, between duty and desire.

As Elara made her way home, her basket filled with the herbs and supplies her father had requested, a sudden sound caught her attention. It was a melody, faint but unmistakable, carried on the breeze from the direction of the forest. The notes were unlike anything she had ever heard, ethereal and enchanting, seeming to weave a spell around her soul.

That's it, she thought, her eyes widening with excitement. *That's the sound I've been searching for!*

Without a second thought, Elara was drawn towards the forest, her feet moving of their own accord. She realized she shouldn't, knew her father would be furious if he found out, but the pull of the music was too strong to resist.

Just a quick look, she told herself as she approached the edge of the trees. *I'll just see where it's coming from and then I'll go straight home.*

But as she stepped into the forest, the melody grew louder, more insistent, as if it were calling to her personally. Elara experienced a thrill of excitement mixed with a tinge of fear. She had never ventured this far into the woods before, had always heeded her father's warnings about the dangers that lurked within.

There was an unspoken law: a large tree that no human from her village was supposed to pass. She was aware that others had been doing so for a long time, but Elara was a good girl and had never gone past it, except once. But the beautiful sound was too strong not to move on.

As she moved deeper into the forest, past the tree, the forest around her seemed to come alive with magic. The trees swayed in time with unheard music, their leaves rustling like whispered secrets. Flowers bloomed in vibrant bursts of color, their petals dancing in the dappled sunlight. Even the air appeared to shimmer with an otherworldly glow as if the very essence of the forest was welcoming her.

This is incredible, Elara thought, her eyes wide with wonder. *It's like a whole other world in here.*

She knew she should turn back, and that she was breaking her promise to her father. But the music was growing louder now and she found herself helpless to resist its call. With each step, she was drawn deeper into the forest's heart, into a world of magic and mystery beyond anything she had ever experienced.

Just a little further, she told herself, even as a small voice warned her to turn back. *Just until I find the source of the music. Then I'll go home, and everything will be fine.*

Chapter 2

LORIEN STALKED THROUGH the forest, his emerald eyes ablaze with fury. The audacity of those humans encroaching upon sacred Faerie lands in their destructive ways. His mother's warnings echoed in his mind—stay away from the boundary line, for that fringe of the woods belonged to the humans now. But he couldn't help himself, drawn by an unseen force to bear witness to their disregard for nature.

He reached the border and halted, his lean muscles tensing beneath his tunic. Before him lay a scene of devastation—proud trees felled by human axes, their trunks brutally hacked and strewn across the mossy ground. Some still bore the marks of human foolishness, initials carved into the bark and encircled by crudely etched hearts. As if their professions of love justified violating a tree.

Lorien knelt, his long fingers tracing footprints pressed into the soft earth. Heavy, ungraceful, so different from the delicate impressions left by Faerie feet. They had no right to be here, trampling through his forest without care or respect.

He rose and gazed around at the carnage, bile rising in his throat. How could they be so short-sighted, so selfish? Did they not realize that the trees were living beings and that harming them upset the balance of the entire forest? Of course, they didn't. Humans never thought of the consequences of their actions.

Lorien's hands balled into fists at his sides, his nails digging into his palms. Someone had to stand up to them to make them see the error of their ways. He was a prince, after all. Perhaps it fell to him to—

But no, his mother had no interest in squabbling with the humans. She said it was pointless as long as they stayed out of the forest.

The problem is that this new generation of humans wasn't listening.

A soft chittering sound drew Lorien's attention, and he turned to see a small squirrel perched on a nearby branch, its bushy tail twitching nervously. Lorien's expression softened, and he approached the creature, humming a gentle melody. The squirrel's ears perked up, responding with urgent chirps and squeaks.

"I know, little friend," Lorien murmured, his voice blending seamlessly with the musical tones. "I see the destruction they've caused. It breaks my heart, too."

The squirrel scurried closer, its tiny claws scratching against the bark. It let out a mournful trill, its dark eyes wide and pleading.

Lorien ran a finger along the squirrel's back, his touch as light as a breeze. "They have no regard for the sanctity of our home," he agreed, his anger simmering beneath the surface. "They think they can take whatever they want without consequence."

The squirrel nuzzled into Lorien's hand, seeking comfort. Lorien's heart ached for the innocent creature and for all the animals who had no choice but to endure humans' recklessness.

"It's not right," he said, his voice hardening. "They've broken the agreement, crossed the line into our territory. They have to be held accountable."

The squirrel chittered in agreement, its tiny body quivering with righteous indignation. Lorien's anger rose to match it, a hot, prickling sensation spreading through his veins like wildfire.

"Something has to be done," he declared, the musical tones of his verbalization to the woodland creature taking on a sharp, discordant edge. "We can't let them get away with this any longer. The humans need to learn their place."

As Lorien's anger reached a crescendo, a sudden rustling in the underbrush caught his attention. The squirrel, startled by the noise, scampered up the tree trunk and disappeared into the foliage. Lorien whirled around, his senses on high alert, ready to confront whatever new threat had invaded his sanctuary.

To his surprise, a young human woman emerged from the bushes, her eyes wide and searching. She was utterly oblivious to Lorien's presence, her gaze darting around the clearing as if looking for something. Lorien observed her warily, his anger momentarily forgotten in the face of this unexpected intrusion.

As the woman drew closer, Lorien couldn't help but note that she was unlike any human he had ever seen before. Her hair was rich, curly and dark, and cascaded over her shoulders.Her hazel eyes were a spark with curiosity. Most of the humans from the local village had long, flat hair like his, but in yellow and sometimes red colors. And her skin was a rich bronze. He hadn't seen any of this color before.

Despite his anger at the humans' transgressions, Lorien begrudgingly admitted that this woman was strangely beautiful. There was something almost otherworldly about her, a quality that set her apart from the other humans he had encountered.

As his eyes followed her through the clearing, Lorien's mind raced with questions. *What was she doing here, so deep in the heart of the Faerie realm? What could she possibly be searching for with such intensity?*

Part of him wanted to confront her, to demand answers and make her pay for the sins of her kind. But another part of him, a part he didn't wholly understand, was drawn to her in a way he had never experienced before.

Lorien shook his head, trying to clear his thoughts. This was no time to be distracted by a pretty face. These humans had violated the agreement and needed to be held accountable. And here, literally, was another violator. No matter how unusual this particular human might be, she was still one of them.

With a deep breath, Lorien stepped out from behind the tree, his anger once again rising to the surface. He would get to the bottom of this intrusion, one way or another. And if this woman was a threat to his beloved forest, he would not hesitate to deal with her accordingly.

Elara's eyes widened as she took in the sight of Lorien, the first faerie she had ever seen in real life. His luminescent markings and silver hair were unlike anything she had ever encountered, and for a moment, she found herself speechless. Despite the tension in the air, she couldn't help but admire his otherworldly beauty.

"Oh, hello there," Elara said, her voice filled with surprise and wonder. She offered a friendly smile, hoping to ease the tension between them. "I'm Elara. I didn't expect to meet anyone out here in the forest."

Lorien's eyes narrowed, his suspicion growing with each passing second. He stepped forward, his gaze fixed on the small blade Elara carried at her side. "What are you doing here, human?" he demanded, his voice cold and accusatory. "And what do you intend to do with that blade? Carve your name into another one of our trees, perhaps?"

Elara's smile faltered, taken aback by the fairy's hostile tone. She glanced down at the blade, realizing how it must have looked to him. "No, no, you've got it all wrong," she said quickly, holding up her hands in a gesture of peace. "I would never harm the forest. I was just out here gathering herbs for my father's shop."

Lorien scoffed, unconvinced by her explanation. "Do you take me for a fool?" he asked, his voice rising with each word. "I know what your kind is capable of. I've seen the destruction you've caused and your disregard for the natural world."

Elara's brow furrowed, a flicker of anger sparking within her. How dare this faerie judge her based on the actions of a few? She opened her mouth to defend herself, but Lorien cut her off before she could speak.

"Don't bother with your excuses," he said, his tone dripping with disdain. "Your presence here is a violation of the agreement between our peoples. You have no right to be in this part of the forest, and I will not stand for any further desecration of our lands."

Elara's eyes widened in disbelief as she processed Lorien's accusation. Her initial awe at encountering a faerie quickly dissipated, replaced by a growing sense of indignation. She straightened her posture and met his gaze head-on, her hazel eyes flickering with stubbornness.

"How dare you accuse me of such a thing!" Elara retorted, her voice rising to match Lorien's. "I would never harm the forest or any of its inhabitants. I was merely gathering herbs for my father's shop, as I've done countless times before."

Lorien's eyes narrowed, his skepticism evident in how his luminescent markings seemed to pulse with each word. "And what of the blade you carry? Do you expect me to believe it's for cutting herbs?"

Elara couldn't help but laugh at the absurdity of his claim. She held out the well-worn knife for Lorien to see. "This? How can I carve my name into a tree with this little thing? It's hardly sharp enough to cut through a stem, let alone bark."

She shook her head, a hint of amusement dancing in her eyes despite the tension between them. "And even if it were sharp enough, I have no lover's name to carve. Unlike some, I don't need to proclaim my affections by defacing nature."

Lorien's brow furrowed, a flicker of irritation crossing his features at her jab. "You dare mock me, human? You know nothing of our ways or the importance we place on preserving the balance of the forest."

Elara's laughter faded, replaced by a steely resolve. "And you know nothing of me or my people. You're so quick to judge, so ready to believe the worst of us based on the actions of a few. It's no wonder there's such distrust between our kinds."

She took a step closer to Lorien, her voice softening but losing none of its intensity. "But I'm not like the others. I respect the forest and all it provides. I would never do anything to harm it or those who call it home."

Lorien's stance remained rigid, his green eyes searching Elara's face for any hint of deception. Deep down, he recognized her words, which held truth, but years of ingrained prejudice and the weight of his duties as a prince made it difficult to accept.

As they stood there, locked in a battle of wills, Elara observed how the sunlight filtered through the canopy, casting a soft glow on Lorien's silver hair. Despite their differences, she found herself drawn to the passion and conviction in his eyes, a mirror of her own. She could tell he cared about the forest. And even if he was being an absolute ass in the way he was showing it, she could respect it.

From a distance, hidden among the foliage, Lorien's faerie friends observed the heated exchange with mixed emotions. Taliesin's dark blue hair twinkling with mischief couldn't suppress a smirk at seeing their usually composed prince engaged in such a spirited debate with a human woman. He twirled a lock of hair around his finger, amused by the unexpected turn of events.

Others, like the fiery-haired Seren, were less entertained. Her eyes narrowed as she watched Elara gesture passionately, her voice carrying through the forest. "How dare she cross into our territory!" Seren hissed, her wings fluttering with agitation. "The audacity of these humans, thinking they can go wherever they please."

Unaware of his friend's presence, Lorien became increasingly frustrated by Elara's stubborn refusal to back down. He clenched his fists at his sides, his voice rising with each word. "You say you're different, but how can I trust that? How can I know you won't betray us like many of your kind have before?"

Elara's eyes flashed with hurt and anger. "I am not responsible for the actions of others. I am my own person, with my own beliefs and values. And I believe in the power of understanding, of finding common ground despite our differences."

She took a deep breath, her voice trembling as she continued. "I came here today not to cause harm but to gather herbs and enjoy the beauty of the forest. Is that so wrong?" For some reason, she hesitated to tell him of the noise she heard that lured her in. He probably wouldn't believe her. "Is it hard to believe a human can appreciate and respect nature?"

Lorien faltered, taken aback by the raw emotion in Elara's words. He looked away, his gaze falling on a nearby tree scarred by human carvings. The sight reignited his anger, and he turned back to Elara with renewed determination.

"Your words are pretty, but they don't change the fact that your kind has repeatedly broken our trust. The damage inflicted on this forest is proof enough of that."

Elara's shoulders sagged, the weight of centuries of conflict bearing down on her. She grasped their argument was about more than her presence in the forest today. It was about the long history of mistrust and misunderstanding between their peoples, a divide that felt impossible to bridge.

Elara reached into her satchel and pulled out a bundle of herbs, holding them out to Lorien. "Look, these are the only things I've taken from the forest today. Herbs for healing, for making medicines to help my people. Herbs for cooking a meal my father is making tonight. I'm not here to destroy or to take more than I need."

Lorien's eyes darted from the herbs to Elara's face, searching for any hint of deception. In her warm, hazel eyes, he saw only sincerity and a glimmer of hope. For a moment, he sensed his resolve waver.

Perhaps she is different, he thought, *perhaps there is a chance for understanding between our kinds.*

But then his gaze fell again on the damaged trees, the scars left by human carelessness and greed. He shook his head, his silver hair catching the dappled sunlight filtering through the canopy.

"It doesn't matter why you're here," he said, his voice cold and unyielding. "Faeries have learned the hard way that humans cannot be trusted. Your presence in our forest violates the agreement between our peoples, and it will not be tolerated."

Elara's eyes glistened with unshed tears, her frustration and disappointment palpable. "So that's it then? You're not even willing to consider that things could be different, that we could find a way to coexist peacefully?"

Lorien's heart ached at the sight of Elara's tears, but he steeled himself against the feeling. *I cannot let her sway me,* he thought, *no matter how much I may want to believe her words.*

"I'm sorry," he said, his voice softening just a bit. "But the safety and well-being of my people must come first. We have suffered too much at the hands of humans to risk opening ourselves up to more harm."

Elara's shoulders slumped. "So what, we just can't come into the forest?" she ask quietly. "Even if what we need is just over this unseen line we've drawn—"

"The line is there for a reason, human."

Elara looked at Lorien, and he impassively looked back. What was a few minutes ago an otherworldly beauty looked cold and heartless.

"Yes, maybe there is a good reason we don't mix," she agreed. She could almost see a flicker of regret pass his face, but he didn't correct her.

"My father was right. Faeries only care about themselves," she added lowly.

Those words did get a reaction. Elara had never seen an angry faerie and immediately hoped she never would again.

Chapter 3

LORIEN GLARED AT ELARA, his green eyes flashing with anger. "I can't believe you would say that!"

He opened his mouth, pointing a thin finger at her. He was about to give her a piece of his mind when he noticed something shift.

Around them, the enchanted forest hummed with energy - the leaves whispering ancient secrets, shafts of golden light painting the mossy ground. Towering trees stretched their gnarled limbs overhead, adorned with luminous flowers that chimed in the gentle breeze. The air was thick with the scent of sweet nectar and earthy petrichor. He sensed the difference but could tell from the human woman's stance that she hadn't.

Elara placed her hands on her hips defiantly. "You think you Faries are better than us because of what—wings? Inborn magic? Long-lives? Good looks?"

Lorien scoffed and shook his head. His eyes looked around the forest, trying to understand the change he sensed. "It's more than that. The magic of this realm must be protected at all costs. As a prince, that is my sole focus."

Deep down, a pang of remorse tugged at Lorien's heart. Elara's wounded expression made him question his harsh words. But his pride and duty to the faerie kingdom kept his temper flared. He couldn't be distracted by a pretty human girl and her alluring voice. He had to figure out what was wrong.

The trees and flowers appeared to lean in as if sensing the crackling tension between the faerie prince and the human bard. Elara straightened her posture, letting the forest's wild magic bolster her confidence without her even realizing it.

"Prince? You're not a prince. You're an ass!"

Suddenly, an invisible force pulled at Elara's chest, causing her to stumble forward. Her eyes widened in surprise as she felt her body moving against her will, drawn towards Lorien like a magnet. "What's happening?" she gasped, her voice tinged with fear and confusion.

Lorien, too, experienced the strange pull, his body moving of its own accord. He tried to resist, planting his feet hard on the ground and straining against the unseen force. "It's some kind of spell," he grunted, his brow furrowed in concentration. "I can feel it."

Elara's heart raced as she struggled to pull away, her fingers clawing at the empty air. She couldn't understand why her body was betraying her, why she was being drawn closer to the infuriating faerie prince. "Make it stop!" she cried, her voice laced with panic.

Lorien's mind raced as he tried to think of how to escape the binding spell. He called upon his own magic, his luminescent markings glowing with a soft silver light. But even his power was useless against this mysterious force. "I'm trying," he said through gritted teeth, his muscles straining.

As they struggled against the spell, Elara and Lorien found themselves face to face, their bodies mere inches apart. Elara's breath caught in her throat as she looked up into Lorien's piercing eyes, seeing the same confusion and frustration reflected back at her. Despite their argument and differences, they were now bound together by this inexplicable magic.

The forest around them hummed with energy, the leaves rustling with a knowing whisper. The air crackled with the power of the spell as if the ancient trees and the earth were conspiring to bring these two unlikely souls together. Elara and Lorien, the human bard and the faerie prince, were caught amid a magical force neither could fight.

Lorien's eyes widened as he realized. "It's a binding spell," he whispered, his voice filled with a mix of awe and trepidation. "Somehow, our argument must have triggered it."

Elara's brows furrowed in confusion. "A binding spell? What does that even mean?" She tried to step back, but her body refused to cooperate. Instead, she stumbled forward, her face nearly colliding with Lorien's chest.

Lorien instantly reached out to steady her, his hands grasping her shoulders. The contact sent a jolt of electricity through both of them, and they quickly pulled apart, only to be drawn back together by the invisible force. "It means," Lorien explained, his voice strained, "that we're stuck together until the spell is broken."

Elara let out a frustrated groan. "Great, just great. Of all the people to be stuck with, it had to be you." She tried to cross her arms, but her elbow accidentally jabbed Lorien in the ribs, causing him to wince.

"Believe me, this isn't my idea of a pleasant situation either," Lorien retorted, rubbing his side. He attempted to step to the side, but Elara's body followed, causing them to bump into each other again.

Elara's foot caught on a tree root as they struggled to find their balance, and she stumbled forward, dragging Lorien with her. They tumbled to the ground in a tangle of limbs, Elara landing on top of Lorien with an "oof!"

For a moment, they lay there, stunned, their faces mere inches apart. Lorien's heart raced beneath Elara's palm, his breath mingling with hers. A blush crept up her cheeks as she realized the intimacy of their position.

Lorien cleared his throat, his own face flushed. "As much as I appreciate your enthusiasm...?"

"Elara."

"Elara. Perhaps we should try to stand up?"

Elara scrambled to her feet, nearly tripping over Lorien in the process. "This is ridiculous," she muttered, brushing leaves and dirt from her clothes. "How are we supposed to go anywhere like this?"

Lorien sighed, running a hand through his silver hair. "We'll have to figure it out. The spell won't break on its own." He looked around the forest, his mind searching for a solution. "Perhaps if we work together, we can find a way to navigate this... situation."

Elara raised an eyebrow, a smirk tugging at her lips. "Work together? That's a tall order, considering we can only just stand next to each other without falling over."

Lorien couldn't help but chuckle at the absurdity of their predicament. "Well, it seems we have no choice. The spell has bound us, for better or worse."

Elara's eyes widened as a realization struck her. "Wait a minute, I need to go home! My father will be worried sick if I don't return soon." She turned to face Lorien, determination etched on her features. "We have to go back to the village now!"

Lorien hesitated, his brows furrowing. "Elara, I don't think that's wise. We don't know the extent of this spell or how it might affect us if we try to separate."

"I don't care!" Elara exclaimed, her frustration mounting. "I can't just disappear without a word. My father, he... he needs me." She took a step towards the direction of the village, but Lorien remained rooted in place.

Elara tugged at the invisible force binding them, her voice rising. "Please. We have to go back."

Lorien shook his head, his voice gentle but firm. "Elara, listen to me. We can't risk making this spell worse. We need to find a way to break it, and I don't think going back to the village is the answer. Besides, I wouldn't step foot into that place."

Elara's shoulders slumped, anger and helplessness washing over her. She looked down at the bundle of herbs and flowers she had collected, her hands trembling. In frustration, she let them fall to the ground, scattering them at her feet.

"Fine," she said, her voice above a whisper. "But if we're not going back, where are we going?"

Lorien glanced deeper into the forest, a pensive look on his face. "There's someone who might be able to help us. An old friend of mine, a wise faerie who knows much about magic."

Elara bit her lip, her mind torn between the desire to return home and the realization that she had no choice but to follow Lorien. With a heavy sigh, she nodded. "Lead the way, then."

As they began to walk deeper into the forest, Elara couldn't shake the unease in her stomach. The further they went, the more the spell pulled, compelling her to stay close to this prince. She glanced over her shoulder, watching as the scattered herbs and flowers disappeared from view, a symbol of the life she was leaving behind to follow this stranger.

The forest felt alive around them as they ventured deeper into its heart. The trees grew taller, their branches intertwining overhead to form a dense canopy that filtered the sunlight into a soft, emerald glow. The air hummed with the gentle whispers of unseen creatures, and the earthy scent of moss and wildflowers filled their nostrils.

Elara couldn't help but marvel at the beauty surrounding her despite the frustration still lingering in her heart. She had always been drawn to the forest, but now, walking beside Lorien, it was different. Magical. It was as if the very essence of the woods was reaching out to her, inviting her to explore its secrets.

The forest Lorien experienced was clearly different than the one she did.

Lorien moved with a purposeful stride, his silver hair catching the dappled light that filtered through the leaves. Elara found herself watching him, studying how his luminescent markings pulsed with each step as if they were connected to the forest's heartbeat.

"How much further?" Elara asked, her voice breaking the silence that had settled between them.

Lorien glanced over his shoulder, his eyes meeting hers briefly. "Not much," he said, his tone softer than before. "We're getting close."

Elara nodded, a small part of her hoping that this wise faerie Lorien spoke of would have the answers they needed. As they continued their journey, the forest shifted around them, the trees parting to reveal hidden paths and clearings that Elara had never seen before.

It was as if the forest itself was guiding them, urging them forward into the unknown. With each step, Elara sensed the pull of the spell growing stronger, the invisible threads that bound her to Lorien tightening their hold.

Elara's mind swirled with conflicting thoughts as she followed Lorien deeper into the enchanted forest. The rational part of her longed to return home to the familiar comfort of her father's cottage and the melodies of her beloved instruments. Yet, another part of her, which had always yearned for adventure and magic, was inexplicably drawn to the mysteries ahead.

"Wait," Elara called out, her voice tinged with frustration. "Can't we just stop for a moment and figure this out? I need to get back home."

Lorien's steps faltered, but he didn't turn to face her. "We can't stop now, Elara. The spell that binds us, it's not something we can ignore."

Elara huffed, her curly dark hair bouncing as she quickened her pace to catch up with him. "But why? Why is this happening to us?"

Lorien remained silent, his stoic demeanor unbreakable as he continued to lead her through the dense foliage. His mind raced with the consequences of their predicament, the weight of his royal status bearing down upon him. What would his people think, seeing their prince tethered to a human? The scandal, the gossip, and the potential diplomatic fallout played out in his mind like a tragic ballad.

Sensing his reluctance to engage, Elara let out a sigh of exasperation. She tapped out a rhythmic pattern on her thigh, a nervous habit she had developed over years of musical practice. The beats seemed to echo through the forest, mingling with the rustling of leaves and the distant trills of exotic birds.

Lost in his thoughts, Lorien barely registered Elara's presence beside him. He quietly cursed the ancient magic that had ensnared them, wondering what cosmic jest had brought a faerie prince and a human woman together in such an impossible situation. The weight of his responsibilities, his people's expectations, and his love for his kingdom all warred within him, leaving him torn and conflicted.

Suddenly, the sound of approaching footsteps and urgent voices broke through the dense foliage, shattering the tense silence that had settled between Elara and Lorien. The faerie prince's eyes widened as he recognized the familiar faces of his friends, their expressions etched with concern and urgency.

"We saw what happened!" said Finnegan, his auburn hair tousled from his swift journey through the forest. "You and the human... you're bound!"

Elara's heart raced as she looked at the approaching faerie. Yesterday she'd never seen a real-live faerie. Now, not only was she tethered to one, but they were literally popping out of the woodwork. She glanced at Lorien, hoping for an explanation, but found only a stoic mask of determination on his face.

Lorien's other friend, Aria, stepped forward, her gossamer wings fluttering nervously. "You must go to the Queen at once," she urged, her melodic voice tinged with worry. "She will know what to do, how to break this spell."

Elara's mind reeled at the mention of the Queen. A faerie queen? She had always believed them to be nothing more than myths and legends, stories whispered by the firelight. And yet, here she was, standing in the heart of an enchanted forest, bound to a faerie prince by a magic she could scarcely comprehend. A prince meant that there must be a queen.

Lorien nodded, his jaw clenched with resolve. "We will go to my mother," he declared, his voice steady despite the turmoil within him. "She will have the answers we seek."

As Lorien stepped forward, Elara felt the invisible force that harnessed them together pull her along like a puppeteer's string. She stumbled along with her frustration and confusion mounting with each passing moment. Lorien's two friends followed along. They were talking, but she wasn't listening.

"Wait!" she cried out, her voice trembling with fear and determination. "I don't understand any of this. I need to go home to my father. He'll be worried sick."

Lorien turned to face her, his green eyes softening with a flicker of understanding. "I know this is not the path you chose..." he said. "But we are bound together now, by a magic that even I do not quite comprehend. We must see this through together."

Elara's heart skipped a beat at the sincerity in Lorien's words. Despite her initial reservations, she was drawn to the faerie prince's quiet strength and the depth of his gaze. With a shaky breath, she nodded, accepting the path that fate had laid before them.

He started walking and, without looking over his shoulder, added, "My name is Lorien, by the way."

"Humph!" was the only reply she gave him. She wouldn't give him the satisfaction of being cordial or acting as if she cared what his name was. Any name he had, he was still an ass to her.

As Lorien and Elara continued their journey deeper into the forest, his friends fell into step behind them.

Elara couldn't help but wonder what she was literally being dragged into.

Chapter 4

"IT WILL BE QUICKER and safer if I carry you," Lorien said, his voice low and melodic. Without waiting for a response, he scooped Elara up into his arms, cradling her against his chest as he took flight.

Elara's breath caught in her throat as she was pressed against Lorien's firm body. The sensation of his strong arms around her, the warmth of his skin through the thin fabric of his tunic, sent a shiver down her spine. She had never been this close to a faerie before, let alone a prince.

As they soared through the air, Elara's mind raced with a whirlwind of thoughts and emotions. She was flying, actually flying, in the arms of a faerie prince. It was like something out of a dream or perhaps a fever-induced hallucination. She wondered if she might wake up at any moment, back in her bed in the village, with this all having been a figment of her overactive imagination.

But the wind whipping through her hair and the solid presence of Lorien's body against hers was all too real. Elara's heart pounded as she realized the gravity of her situation. She was not only in the arms of a faerie prince, but somehow physically attached to him. The implications of this slowly began to dawn on her, causing a wave of confusion and disbelief to wash over her.

"Lorien, what's happening?" Elara asked, her voice rising with fear. "Why can't I move away from you? Where are you taking me?"

Lorien glanced down at her, his green eyes glinting with a mix of concern and determination. "I'm taking you to the heart of my kingdom where we'll figure this out. I promise."

Elara swallowed hard, trying to process this information. Bound together by a spell? With a faerie prince? It was almost too much to comprehend. And now she was being brought into the very heart of the Faerie kingdom, a place she had only heard about in stories and legends.

Lorien's two friends flew ahead, showing off a feat of acrobatic aerial skills that caught her attention, briefly distracting her from the fact that she was soaring above the trees.

As they flew onward, Elara couldn't help but marvel at the beauty of the world below her, despite her tumultuous emotions. The forest stretched out in a sea of vibrant greens, punctuated by the glittering silver of rivers and streams. In the distance, she could see the spires and turrets of what could only be the faerie palace, rising up like a dream against the horizon. From her village she couldn't see anything of the world of the Faries.

Elara took a deep breath, trying to steady herself. Whatever lay ahead, she knew she would have to face it with courage and resilience. She was Elara Mariposa Santiago, after all. She had never backed down from a challenge before, and she wasn't about to start now, even if that challenge involved being magically bound to a faerie prince in the heart of his kingdom.

As they approached the palace, Elara's eyes widened in wonder. The faerie kingdom was even more breathtaking up close, with its shimmering walls and intricate architecture that seemed to defy the laws of physics. The air hummed with a palpable energy, and Elara sensed magic thrumming through her veins, as if the very essence of the place was calling out to her.

Lorien began to descend, his wings beating in a steady rhythm as they approached a grand terrace that jutted out from the palace walls. With a graceful touch, he landed on the smooth stone surface.

The moment they touched the ground, Elara tried to step away from Lorien, eager to put some distance between them after the intimate proximity of their flight. To her surprise and dismay, she found that she couldn't move more than a foot away from him, as if an invisible force was holding them together.

"This is ridiculous..." Elara muttered, her brow furrowing in confusion as she tried again to step away, only to be pulled back towards Lorien like a magnet.

Lorien, too, looked taken aback by this development. He attempted to move in the opposite direction but found himself similarly restricted. "It appears the binding spell is more...comprehensive than I initially thought," he said, his voice tinged with a mix of frustration and embarrassment.

Elara couldn't help but let out a small, incredulous laugh at the absurdity of their situation. Here she was, in the heart of the faerie kingdom, magically bound to a prince who, until recently, she had believed to be nothing more than a myth. It was like something out of a bizarre dream.

"Well, this is just great," she said, her tone dripping with sarcasm. "Not only am I stuck with you, but I can't even get a moment's peace to process all of this."

Lorien's face flushed, and he opened his mouth to retort, but before he could speak, the sound of approaching footsteps caught their attention. Elara turned to see a group of fairies emerging from the palace, including his two friends who had taken off ahead of them. The group was led by a regal-looking woman with silver hair and piercing blue eyes.

The woman's gaze fell upon Elara and Lorien, and a small, amused smile tugged at the corners of her lips. "Well, well," she said, her voice rich and melodic. "It seems we have a most unusual situation on our hands."

Elara straightened her spine, determined not to show any weakness or intimidation in the face of this new challenge. The woman looked strikingly like Lorien. She didn't need to take a far leap to realize she was his mother—the Queen.

Beside the Queen stood a younger faerie with platinum hair and ice-blue eyes, her ethereal beauty almost as striking as the Queen's. She observed the scene with a mixture of curiosity and amusement, her gaze flickering between Elara and Lorien.

"Mother," Lorien began, his voice strained with embarrassment, "this is not what it looks like. We've been—"

"Bound by the ancient spell, yes, I know," the Queen interrupted, her eyes twinkling with mirth. "Your friends arrived just before you and explained the situation."

Elara's brows furrowed in confusion. "Ancient spell? What ancient spell?"

The Queen turned her attention to Elara, her expression softening. "It is a spell that was created long ago to foster understanding between our kinds. It binds a faerie and a human together until they truly comprehend one another."

"But why us?" Elara asked, frustration seeping into her voice. "We didn't ask for this!"

"The spell is triggered by strong emotions, particularly anger and hatred," the platinum-haired faerie chimed in, her voice soft and melodic. "It seems that your feelings towards each other were intense enough to activate it."

Lorien's face reddened, and he looked away, clearly uncomfortable with the implications of the fairy's words. Elara, too, had a rush of embarrassment, but she refused to let it show. She couldn't have feelings, much less strong ones, for someone she'd just met.

"The spell can only be triggered near the border between your village and our realm," the Queen explained, her voice calm and patient. "The more you fight against it, the closer it will force you to be. At the very least, you must remain within a few feet of each other until you really understand and accept one another. Sometimes closer, sometimes further. The distance permitted is up to you."

Elara's mind reeled at the thought of being so close to Lorien for an indefinite period. She glanced at him, noticing the way his jaw clenched and his eyes narrowed. He clearly wasn't thrilled about the prospect either. And as if in answer, there was a a slight tug at both and the found themselves about an inch closer together. The faerie next to the Queen chuckled.

"This is not funny, Aria," Lorien looked at her. But the faerie didn't seem the least intimidated. In fact, she laugh out loud. Lorien looked at Elara and grimaced. The two slid another inch closer, and Aria let out a howl of laughter that bounced off the walls of the room.

The Queen gave her a side look to simmer down, though her own face also reflected amusement.

"But why were you in our part of the forest?" the Queen asked, her gaze curious. "It's not often that we find humans wandering so close to our borders."

Elara felt her cheeks warm as she recalled the enchanting melody that had drawn her deeper into the woods. "I heard the most beautiful sounds," she admitted, her voice soft with wonder. "It was like nothing I'd ever heard before, and I couldn't help but follow it."

Beside her, Lorien stiffened, his eyes widening in what appeared to be horror. He opened his mouth as if to say something, but Elara continued, lost in the memory.

"It was like the forest itself was singing, and I experienced this incredible sense of peace and belonging. I've never experienced anything like it."

The Queen's eyes sparkled with amusement, and she glanced at Lorien, who looked as though he wished the ground would swallow him whole. "Is that so?" she mused, her tone light and teasing. "It seems you have quite the admirer, Lorien."

Elara's brows furrowed in confusion, but before she could ask what the Queen meant, Lorien spoke up, his voice strained. "Mother, please. Can we focus on the matter at hand?"

The Queen chuckled but nodded, her expression growing more serious. "Of course. We must find a way to help you both navigate this situation until the spell is broken."

As the conversation turned to practical matters, Elara couldn't help but wonder about the Queen's cryptic words. What did she mean about Lorien having an admirer? And why had he been so embarrassed by her description of the music in the forest?

She glanced at him from the corner of her eye, taking in the tense set of his shoulders and the way his balled-up hands hung by his thigh. Despite her frustration with the situation, she couldn't help but feel a twinge of sympathy for him. This couldn't be easy for him either, being bound to a human he clearly despised.

But as she listened to the Queen and Lorien discuss the logistics of their predicament, Elara found herself growing more and more intrigued by the faerie prince. There was something about him, beneath the haughty exterior and the sharp tongue, that called to her. And now, with the spell forcing them together, she had a feeling she was about to discover just what that something was.

Lorien shifted uncomfortably, his brow furrowed as he addressed his mother. "What about...personal matters? Sleeping arrangements, bathing?" He cast a sidelong glance at Elara, his discomfort palpable. "Surely you don't expect me to share my private quarters with a human?"

Queen Sylvana's eyes sparkled with amusement, but she maintained a composed demeanor. "I understand your concerns, Lorien. We will make the necessary accommodations to ensure both of your comfort and privacy." She turned to Elara, her voice warm and reassuring. "I apologize for the inconvenience this may cause you, Elara. Please know that we will do our best to make your stay here as pleasant as possible, given the circumstances."

Elara nodded, trying to mask her own apprehension. The thought of being in such close proximity to Lorien, even in the most mundane of situations, sent a mixture of nervousness and anticipation coursing through her. She mentally chided herself for the latter, reminding herself that this was a prince who had made his disdain for humans quite clear.

Lorien, however, was far from placated. "Pleasant? Mother, this is hardly a situation that can be described as pleasant." He ran a hand through his silver hair, frustration etched on his handsome features. "I have duties, responsibilities. How am I supposed to fulfill them while tethered to a human?"

The Queen placed a comforting hand on her son's shoulder. "We will find a way, Lorien. This spell, while inconvenient, is an opportunity for growth and understanding." Her gaze drifted to Elara, a knowing smile playing at the corners of her lips. "For both of you."

A blush crept up Elara's neck at the Queen's words. She may not have chosen this path, but she would face it with the same courage and resilience that had gotten her through countless challenges before.

As if sensing her resolve, Lorien sighed, his posture relaxing slightly. "Very well. I trust you will make the necessary arrangements, Mother." He turned to Elara, his green eyes intense. "I suppose we have no choice but to make the best of this situation."

Elara couldn't help but smile at his grudging acceptance. "I suppose we don't." She held out her hand, a peace offering. "Truce?"

Lorien stared at her outstretched hand for a moment, before reaching out and grasping it. "Truce."

As their hands touched, a spark of something pass between them, a flicker of the magic that now bound them together. She met Lorien's gaze, seeing her own surprise mirrored in his eyes.

Perhaps, she thought, this unexpected journey would lead them to more than just a resolution to the spell. Perhaps it would lead them to a deeper understanding of each other, and of themselves.

Aria stepped forward, her ethereal presence drawing everyone's attention. "I will research the spell and see if I can find any information on how it might be broken," she offered, her voice soft and melodic. "It may take some time, but I will do my best to assist you both."

Elara's playful nature couldn't resist the opportunity to tease Lorien further. With a mischievous glint in her hazel eyes, she quipped, "Maybe it's something silly, like a true love's kiss. Wouldn't that be a twist?"

Lorien's eyes widened, a mix of embarrassment and horror washing over his handsome features. He quickly composed himself, but not before Elara caught the hint of a blush on his cheeks. She found his discomfort endearing, and her smile only grew wider.

Queen Sylvana and Aria exchanged amused glances, their eyes dancing with mirth at Lorien's predicament. This time it was the Queen's laughter that rang out like a gentle melody, filling the throne room with its warmth.

Aria, however, couldn't resist adding her own insight. "The spell was not intended to make people fall in love," she clarified, her tone both informative and teasing. "It is unlikely that Lorien would have to develop romantic feelings for Elara for the spell to be broken."

Elara found herself oddly disappointed by this revelation, though she couldn't quite pinpoint why. She shook off the thought, focusing instead on the amusement shared by everyone in the room except for Lorien.

The faerie prince stood tall, his posture regal despite the awkwardness of the situation. His green eyes darted between Elara, his mother, and Aria, as if trying to gauge their reactions. Elara could almost see the gears turning in his head as he grappled with the implications of their predicament.

As the laughter subsided, Queen Sylvana clapped her hands together, drawing everyone's attention. "Well, it seems we have much to discuss and arrange," she said, her tone both authoritative and compassionate. "Lorien, Elara, why don't you take a moment to catch your breath on the terrace while I confer with Aria? We will reconvene shortly to discuss the next steps."

Lorien nodded, his relief evident in the way his shoulders relaxed. He turned to Elara, offering his arm in a gentlemanly gesture. "Shall we?"

Elara hesitated for a moment, the reality of their situation sinking in. She was bound to Lorien, a faerie prince, in a world she had only ever dreamed of. The weight of it all threatened to overwhelm her, but she took a deep breath, pushing down her doubts and fears.

With a smile that was both nervous and excited, she took Lorien's arm, allowing him to guide her towards the terrace. As they walked, she couldn't help but marvel at the way his skin glowed in the soft light, the markings on his face and arms shimmering like stardust.

Perhaps, she thought, this unexpected journey would lead them to more than just a resolution to the spell. Perhaps it would lead them to a deeper understanding of each other, and of themselves.

Chapter 5

ELARA TWIRLED AS SHE stepped out into the sunlight, her dark curls bouncing with each playful step. She breathed in the fresh air, relishing the scents of wildflowers and the earthy aroma of the forest. Beside her, Lorien walked with a measured gait, his silver hair catching the light like a halo.

"Come on, your highness," Elara teased, her hazel eyes sparkling with mischief. "Don't tell me you've forgotten how to have fun in these woods of yours."

Lorien arched an eyebrow, his luminescent markings shimmering faintly. "I assure you, Lady Elara, I am quite capable of enjoyment. It's just that some of us prefer a more refined approach."

Elara laughed, the sound ringing through the glade like a melody. "Lady? I like the sound of that. And is that what you call it? Refined? I think you might need a lesson or two in letting loose."

She spun around him, her skirts swishing against the grass. Lorien eyed her, a smile tugging at the corner of his lips despite himself. Something about Elara's carefree spirit was infectious, chipping away at the formal exterior he'd so carefully cultivated.

"And I suppose you fancy yourself the teacher for such lessons?" he countered, a hint of playfulness creeping into his tone.

Elara grinned, her eyes dancing with a challenge. "Oh, I don't know. I might have a trick or two up my sleeve. The real question is, are you brave enough to find out?"

She raised her chin, meeting his gaze with a mischievous glint. Lorien felt a strange flutter in his chest, a warmth that had nothing to do with the sun overhead. He couldn't help but be drawn to her vibrant energy, so different from the reserved interactions he was accustomed to.

"I accept your challenge, my lady," he said with a mock bow. "Lead the way, and let us see what mischief you have in store."

Elara clapped her hands in delight, her smile radiant. "Now that's more like it! Stick with me, Your Highness, and I'll show you a side of these woods you've never seen before."

"Stick with you?" he said, just a few paces behind. "I have no choice."

Elara's mind wandered to her greatest passion as they continued their stroll. "You know, Lorien, there's nothing quite like music to make the soul come alive," she mused, her voice taking on a dreamy quality. "The way a melody can transport you, the emotions it can evoke... it's pure magic. I heard tales that your people have some amazing musicians. Do you think I might meet one while I'm here?"

Lorien's interest was piqued by her words, and he was drawn into the conversation. "I'm sure that could be arranged," he replied, his own love for music shining through. "Tell me, Elara, what genres of music captivate you the most?"

Elara's face lit up. "Oh, I love it all! From the lively jigs and reels that make you want to dance until your feet ache to the haunting ballads that tug at your heartstrings. But there's something special about the music of the forest, the way it seems to whisper secrets and weave spells around you."

Lorien nodded, understanding her sentiment all too well. "The music of nature is indeed powerful. The rustle of leaves, the chirping of birds, the babbling of brooks all contribute to a symphony that is both ancient and ever-changing."

As they exchanged stories of their favorite instruments and musical experiences, Lorien marveled at the depths of Elara's passion. Her eyes sparkled with joy as she recounted tales of impromptu jam sessions and the thrill of mastering a new song. At that moment, he saw a kindred spirit who understood music's transformative power.

Suddenly, a thought struck Elara, and her brow furrowed in confusion. "Lorien, I've been meaning to ask you... You started acting strange when I mentioned the beautiful sound that lured me into the forest. Is everything alright?"

Lorien's steps faltered for a moment, and he averted his gaze. "It's nothing, really," he said with a shrug, trying to brush off the topic. "I didn't hear anything out of the ordinary."

But Elara was not easily deterred. She gently touched his arm, sending a jolt through him. "Are you sure? You seemed... unsettled. If there's something on your mind, you can tell me."

Lorien hesitated, a flicker of uncertainty in his eyes. He wasn't used to sharing his thoughts so freely, especially with someone he'd only met.

"It's just... the idea of a sound luring you into the forest; it reminds me of old tales I've heard. Tales of enchantments and fate magic." He shook his head, trying to dispel the unease that had crept into his mind. "But it's probably nothing. Just my imagination running wild."

Elara studied him for a moment, her gaze thoughtful. "Well, whatever it was, I'm glad it led me to you," she said tenderly, her words carrying a weight that made Lorien's heart skip a beat. When he looked at her, the realization of the words came to her, and she rushed on, "I wouldn't have ever seen this place if I hadn't run into your moody highness. And if some strange magic is at play, we'll have to face it together."

"Together, together," he drudged, following slowly. He wasn't used to so much walking. "Yes, together."

Elara smiled warmly at Lorien, her eyes sparkling with understanding. "Why don't we find a quiet spot to sit and talk more? I'd love to hear about your musical journey, and maybe we can find some common ground."

Lorien nodded, a small smile tugging at the corners of his lips. "I'd like that."

They wandered through the lush forest until they came across a large oak tree, its branches stretching like welcoming arms. The dappled sunlight filtering through the leaves created a serene, intimate atmosphere. Elara led the way, settling down on the soft grass beneath the tree and patting the spot beside her.

As Lorien lowered himself to the ground, he noted how close they were, their shoulders nearly touching. A flutter of nervousness danced in his stomach, but he was drawn to Elara's warmth and openness.

"So, tell me about your musical journey," Elara prompted, her eyes filled with genuine interest. "What inspired you to pursue music?"

Lorien leaned back against the sturdy trunk of the oak, his gaze drifting upward as he gathered his thoughts. "Music has always been a part of me, woven into the very fabric of my being," he began, his voice soft and contemplative. "In our realm, music is more than just sound; it's a connection to the natural world, a way to communicate with the forest and all its inhabitants."

Elara listened intently, her head tilted as she absorbed his words. "That sounds incredible," she breathed, her passion for music shining through. "Music has been a constant companion, a way to express my emotions and tell stories. It's like a language that transcends boundaries and brings people together."

As they continued to share their experiences, Lorien found himself opening up in ways he never had before. He spoke of the challenges he faced as a prince, the expectations placed upon him, and how music provided solace and freedom. Elara, in turn, shared her dreams of performing for the royal families, the obstacles she had overcome, and the joy she found in creating melodies that touched people's hearts.

"How do you come up with ideas for your songs?" he asked, watching the sunlight play off her curls.

Elara waved her hands dismissively. "They just come to me. Life, things happen... then the music comes."

Elara's eyes sparkled with mischief as she turned to face Lorien. "How about a little game?" she suggested, her voice carrying a playful lilt. "We take turns humming a melody, and the other has to guess the song. I think if we stick to old classic songs that both of our people have had for a while, you might stand a chance of beating me. Think you're up for the challenge, Prince Lorien?"

Lorien arched an eyebrow, a hint of a smile tugging at the corners of his lips. "I accept your challenge, Lady Elara," he replied in an equally playful tone. "But be warned, I have an extensive knowledge of melodies from both our realms."

Elara grinned, undeterred by his confident demeanor. She closed her eyes briefly, gathering her thoughts before humming a soft, enchanting tune that seemed to dance on the gentle breeze. Lorien listened intensively. His brow furrowed in concentration as he tried to place the familiar melody.

"Ah, 'The Ballad of the Moonlit Glade,' " he declared triumphantly, a smile spreading across his face. "A classic from the faerie realm, known for its hauntingly beautiful harmonies."

Elara clapped her hands in delight, impressed by his quick recognition. "Well done, Prince Lorien," she praised, her eyes twinkling with admiration. "Your turn now."

Lorien took a deep breath, his eyes drifting skyward as he searched for the perfect melody. He began to hum a lively, energetic tune, his foot tapping in time with the imagined beat. Elara's face scrunched up in concentration, her mind racing to identify the song.

"Oh, I know this one!" she exclaimed, snapping her fingers. "'The Dance of the Fireflies,' a popular tune among the human villages during the summer festivals."

Lorien nodded, impressed by her knowledge. "Indeed, Lady Elara. You have a keen ear for music."

As they continued their game, their laughter filled the air, echoing through the tranquil forest. They took turns humming melodies from both the faerie and human realms, each trying to stump the other with obscure tunes and challenging rhythms. The competitive spirit between them was tempered by their joy in sharing their love for music.

He's not as aloof as I thought, Elara mused, watching Lorien's face light up with genuine enjoyment. *There's a warmth to him, a depth beyond his noble bearing.*

Just as Elara was about to take her turn, a servant approached them, bowing respectfully. "Your Highness, Lady Elara," the servant addressed them, "the Queen has finished preparing your shared living quarters. She invites you to return and settle in for the evening."

Lorien and Elara exchanged glances, a flicker of anticipation passing between them. "Thank you," Lorien replied, rising gracefully to his feet and offering his hand to Elara. "Shall we, Lady Elara?"

Elara accepted his hand, a slight flush coloring her cheeks as she stood up. "Lead the way, Prince Lorien," she replied, her voice soft and filled with a newfound warmth.

As they returned to the palace, their steps fell into sync, a silent acknowledgment of their growing bond. The setting sun painted the sky in hues of gold and pink, casting a warm glow over their figures. Elara found herself stealing glances at Lorien, admiring how fading light danced across his luminescent markings.

As they entered their shared living quarters, Elara and Lorien couldn't help but chuckle at the attempts to provide them privacy. A thin, gauzy curtain had been hung across the center of the room, creating two separate spaces that were more symbolic than practical. The beds on either side of the curtain were so close they could easily reach out and touch each other.

"Well, this is cozy," Elara remarked, her eyes sparkling with amusement as she surveyed the room. "I guess we'll have to be mindful of our movements, or we might end up in each other's laps."

Lorien's lips twitched into a smile, his green eyes glinting with mirth. "Indeed, Lady Elara. It seems the concept of personal space will be a luxury in these quarters."

As they navigated the small room, their movements were marked by awkward bumps and apologetic smiles. Occasionally, they sensed the spell pulling them closer, reminding them that the proximity was more than a choice, but a mythical mandate. Elara reached for her bag, accidentally brushing against Lorien's arm, while he turned to hang his cloak, nearly colliding with her in the process.

This is going to be an interesting adventure, Elara thought, suppressing a giggle as Lorien try to find a place to put his belongings without invading her space.

In an attempt to feel at home, Elara picked up a vase of flowers from a small table and intended to move it to her bedside. However, as she turned, her elbow accidentally knocked the vase, sending it tumbling to the floor. Water and flowers spilled across the stone, creating a puddle at their feet.

"Oh, no!" Elara gasped, immediately dropping to her knees to pick up the scattered blooms. "I'm so sorry. I can be such a klutz sometimes."

Lorien knelt beside her, his hands brushing against hers as he helped gather the flowers. "It's quite alright, Lady Elara. Accidents happen," he reassured her, his voice soft and understanding.

As they worked together to clean up the mess, their hands continued to touch, lingering for a moment longer than necessary. A warmth spread through her, a tingling sensation that had nothing to do with the cool water on her skin.

There's something about him, she mused, sneaking a glance at Lorien as he carefully arranged the salvaged flowers in the vase. *A gentleness, a depth of empathy that I didn't expect.*

With the mess cleaned up and the vase safely placed on the table, Elara and Lorien found themselves standing close, their eyes locked in a moment of unexpected tenderness. The air between them tense.

It was bedtime.

"I'll turn my back," Lorien said, gesturing for Elara to head to the wardrobe full of clothing for her that had been placed in the room.

She opened it and gasped. Fairies, especially royal ones, sure knew how to dress. She peeked at the back and saw someone had even stitched up the opening for the wings so her bare back wouldn't be exposed.

She cast a glance over her shoulder. Lorien was still turned away but was rocking impatiently on his heels.

When Lorien heard clothing hit the ground as she undressed to slip into a nightgown, he wanted to turn around and see.

Was she that beautiful bronze color all over? Where the curls on her head... well, was all her hair curly?

But he didn't turn around. He just listened to her hum absent-mindedly as she changed.

"Done," she said a few moments later.

He turned to see her in a long green silk sleeping slip. He wanted to roll his eyes. His mother could have given her a cotton cloth or tunic and pants. But no, she had given the human woman that—a slip that hugged every curve that Lorien had only imagined until that point.

He must have been staring because Elara flushed, then rushed into her bed and pulled the covers up. She turned her back. "Your turn."

Lorien sighed. This was never going to work. It took all his effort to take a step toward his wardrobe. A moment later, he slipped into his bed and turned his back to her as well.

Elara's soft voice broke the silence as the candlelight flickered, casting dancing shadows on the walls. "Lorien, what do you hope for in life?" Her question hung in the air, a gentle invitation for him to open up.

Lorien shifted, turning to face her. His green eyes glowed in the dim light as he considered her question. "I hope to make a difference in my realm, to be a leader who brings harmony and understanding between our people and the natural world." He paused, his voice growing more vulnerable. "But sometimes, I fear I may not be up to the task, that I might fail those who depend on me."

Elara sat up, her hazel eyes filled with empathy. "I understand that fear," she confided. "I've always dreamed of becoming a musician for a royal family, just like my mother. But my father..." She trailed off, her gaze falling to her hands. "He wants me to follow a different path, one that keeps me far away from the faerie folk."

Lorien's brow furrowed, curiosity mingling with concern. "Why does your father hate the faerie folk so much?" he asked, hoping to understand the root of the conflict.

Elara's shoulders tensed, and she shook her head. "It's a long story, one I'm not ready to tell." Her voice was just above a whisper, the weight of her father's resentment hanging heavy in the air.

They both heard the scrap as their beds were pulled together ever so slightly. Both ignored it or at least tried.

Sensing her discomfort, Lorien changed the subject. "Tell me more about your dreams of being a royal musician," he encouraged, his voice warm and inviting. "What inspired you to pursue that path?"

A small smile played on Elara's lips as she recalled the memories. "My mother's music was magical. She would weave emotions into her melodies, bringing joy and solace to all who heard her play." Her eyes sparkled with admiration. "I want to create that same magic, to touch people's hearts with my music."

Lorien found himself drawn to her passion, the way her whole being lit up when she spoke of music. "I do not doubt that you will achieve your dreams, Elara," he said softly, his words filled with genuine belief in her abilities.

As the night wore on, when they should have been sleeping, every now and again, Elara would ask Lorien a question, and he'd turn over and look at her in the amber hue of the candlelight and was compelled to answer.

As the candle burned low and their eyelids grew heavy, Elara and Lorien bid each other goodnight. They drifted off to sleep, a mere foot apart, still wondering how they could bridge the chasm between them to break the spell.

Chapter 6

LORIEN GLIDED THROUGH the halls of the Great Willow, his luminescent markings casting a soft glow on the polished bark walls. Elara trailed behind him, her footsteps echoing in the quiet space. She sighed, her boredom palpable as they moved from one meeting to another.

"Can we take a break?" Elara asked, her voice tinged with frustration. "We've been at this for hours, and I look like a shadow following you around."

Lorien paused, turning to face her with a raised eyebrow. "Elara, these meetings are crucial for the well-being of the faerie realm. I understand it may not be the most thrilling way to spend your time, but it is necessary."

Elara frowned, crossing her arms over her chest. "I get that, but do I need to be here for all of them? Can't you skip a few? I'm just sitting in the back, not allowed to say anything or contribute. It's frustrating."

Lorien's eyes softened, but his tone remained firm. "It is only proper, Elara. As a human woman, it would be inappropriate to voice your opinions on matters that solely concern the fairies."

A flash of hurt crossed Elara's face, and she looked away, biting her lip to avoid retorting. The binding spell pulsed between them, and Lorien experienced the tug pulling them closer together, now only a hand's breadth apart.

I didn't mean to upset her, Lorien thought, a twinge of guilt flickering through him. *But she must understand her place here. The faerie council would never accept a human's input.*

Elara remained silent, her gaze fixed on the intricate patterns woven into the floor. Tension hung heavy in the air between them, and the only sound was the soft rustling of leaves outside the windows.

Lorien sighed, running a hand through his silver hair. "Elara, I apologize if my words came across as harsh. I did not intend to diminish your worth or suggest that you are unimportant."

She glanced up at him, her hazel eyes glistening with unshed tears. "I understand my place, Lorien. I just... I'm so useless, like I'm nothing more than a burden you're forced to carry around. I miss home. I'm worried about my father and brother..."

The spell tugged at them again, and Lorien reached out, his hand grabbing hers in a gesture of comfort. "You are not a burden, Elara. Your presence here, while unexpected, has brought a new perspective to my life. I am grateful for that, even if I may not always show it. And we're working to return you to your life as quickly as possible."

A small smile tugged at the corners of Elara's mouth, and she let her fingers intertwine with his briefly before pulling away. "Thank you, Lorien. That means a lot to me."

Lorien cleared his throat, eager to move past the emotionally charged moment. "Well, since my duties for the day are concluded, perhaps we could find a more enjoyable way to pass the time together."

Elara's eyes lit up, a mischievous grin spreading across her face. "I have an idea! Let's play hide-and-seek in the forest."

Hide-and-seek? With the spellbinding us so closely? That's ridiculous, Lorien thought to himself, but seeing the excitement dancing in Elara's eyes, he couldn't bring himself to voice his doubts. Instead, he nodded, a small smile playing on his lips. "Very well, Elara. Lead the way."

Hand in hand, they ventured into the forest, the dappled sunlight filtering through the canopy above. Elara's laughter rang out, a melodic sound that harmonized with the whisper of the wind through the leaves. "I'll hide first," she declared, releasing Lorien's hand and darting behind a nearby tree.

Lorien shook his head, amused by her enthusiasm. He dutifully closed his eyes and began counting aloud, "One, two, three..."

As he counted, he heard Elara's muffled giggles and the rustle of her skirts as she attempted to find a suitable hiding spot within the confines of the spell's reach. *This is utterly absurd,* he thought, *but if it brings her joy, I suppose I can endure it.*

"...eight, nine, ten! Ready or not, here I come!" Lorien called out, opening his eyes and scanning his surroundings. He spotted a flash of Elara's vibrant dress peeking out from behind a bush and grinned, making his way towards her.

Elara squealed in delight as Lorien approached, leaping out from her hiding spot and darting away. "Catch me if you can!" she taunted, laughter echoing through the trees.

Lorien found himself caught up in the moment, chasing after her with a newfound sense of playfulness. It had been a while since he just played. Most people were too formal around him to enjoy himself. And he had little time to spend with the few friends he had. As they wove between the trees, their laughter mingling with the birdsong above, the spell's invisible tether ensured they were never more than a few steps apart.

As they played, the weight of his responsibilities and the strain of their predicament melted away, replaced by a carefree joy Lorien had not experienced in centuries. *Perhaps,* he mused, *there is more to this human than I initially believed.*

Suddenly, Elara's foot caught on a gnarled tree root, and she stumbled forward with a gasp. Instinctively, Lorien lunged to catch her, his arms encircling her waist as she fell against his chest. For a brief moment, they stood frozen, their faces mere inches apart, their breath mingling in the space between them.

Elara's hazel eyes widened, a faint blush coloring her cheeks as she realized the intimacy of their position. Lorien, too, felt a stirring in his chest.

Then, as quickly as the moment had arrived, it passed. Elara burst into laughter, her eyes crinkling with mirth. "Well, that was quite the tumble!" she exclaimed, untangling herself from Lorien's embrace. "I suppose I should be more mindful of where I step."

Lorien was chuckling along with her, the tension dissipating like morning mist. "Indeed, we can't have you injuring yourself on my watch. My reputation as a guardian would be tarnished forever."

Lorien's gaze drifted to a narrow path winding through the trees as their laughter subsided. "Come," he said, offering Elara his hand. "There's something I'd like to show you."

Curiosity piqued, Elara accepted his outstretched hand, allowing him to guide her along the path. They walked in comfortable silence, the spell humming faintly between them until the trees parted to reveal a hidden meadow.

Elara gasped in wonder, her eyes widening at the sight before her. The meadow was a sea of vibrant wildflowers, their petals dancing in the gentle breeze. Butterflies flitted from blossom to blossom, their delicate wings catching the sunlight. Some of the butterflies looked like the ones she was used to. But there were a few that she'd never seen. The most captivating ones flapped large wings that looked like they were made of stained glass.

"Lorien, this is... breathtaking," she whispered, her voice filled with awe.

Lorien smiled, a flicker of pride in his eyes. "I discovered this place decades ago, during a particularly trying time in my life. It has served as a sanctuary ever since."

He led her to the meadow's center, where they settled among the flowers, allowing them to recline comfortably side by side. For a while, they lay there, basking in the tranquility of their surroundings, the scent of the blooms enveloping them like a soothing balm.

As the sun moved across the horizon, Elara turned to Lorien, her expression softening. "Tell me about your childhood," she said, her tone gentle. "I'd love to know more about the man behind the guardian."

Lorien hesitated for a moment. But Elara's open, inviting demeanor made him want to trust her and let her see a side of him that few others had.

As the afternoon stretched on, Lorien found himself sharing stories from his youth—tales of mischief and adventure, lessons learned, and bonds forged. In turn, Elara regaled him with anecdotes from her own childhood, painting a picture of a young girl with a love for music and a thirst for knowledge.

The barriers between them felt like they melted away as they spoke, replaced by a growing sense of understanding and connection. They were not a faerie prince and a human woman bound by a mysterious spell for a few precious hours but simply two souls finding solace in each other's company.

Lorien mused, watching the fading sunlight play across Elara's features. *Perhaps a faerie could have more in common with a human than he initially thought.*

Elara's eyes sparkled with a playful glint. She rose to her feet, brushing stray blades of grass from her skirt, and turned to Lorien with a mischievous smile.

"I challenge you to a race," she declared, her voice ringing excitedly. "The first one to reach that big oak tree at the meadow's edge wins."

Lorien arched an eyebrow, a smirk tugging at the corner of his lips. "A race? Are you sure you want to challenge a faerie to a test of speed?"

Elara's grin only widened. "Afraid you might lose, Your Highness?"

Her audacity is as refreshing as it is surprising, Lorien thought, chuckling softly. Out loud, he said, "Very well, I accept your challenge. But don't say I didn't warn you."

They took their positions at the edge of the meadow, shoulders nearly brushing, the air between them crackling with anticipation. "Ready?" Elara asked, her body coiled like a spring.

Lorien nodded, his own muscles tensing in preparation. "Set..."

"Go!" they shouted in unison, and then they were off, sprinting through the forest, their laughter mingling with the rhythmic pounding of their feet against the earth.

The world around them became a blur of greens and gold, the wind whipping through their hair as they raced neck and neck. Elara's skirt billowed behind her, her laughter ringing out like a melody, while Lorien's movements were fluid and graceful, his body attuned to the pulse of the forest.

Lorien marveled, glancing at Elara as they wove between the trees. *She's fast. And her joy... it's infectious.*

As they neared the finish line, Lorien held back, allowing Elara to pull ahead just enough to touch the oak tree a split second before he did. Her triumphant whoop echoed through the forest, and she turned to him, her eyes alight with victory.

"I won!" she exclaimed, her chest heaving with exertion, her smile brighter than the sun.

Unable to resist her infectious enthusiasm, Lorien broke into a grin. "So you did," he conceded, bowing his head in acknowledgment. "Well raced, Elara."

As their laughter subsided, Lorien's expression grew thoughtful. He looked up at the sun, appearing to try to calculate time. "Come with me," he said, holding out his hand. "There's something else I want to show you."

Elara, her curiosity piqued, placed her hand in his, marveling at the way his warm, strong fingers curled around hers. *Where is he taking me?* she wondered, her heart fluttering with a mix of anticipation and something she couldn't quite name.

Lorien led her through the forest. The sound of rushing water grew louder, and as they stepped into a clearing, Elara gasped, her eyes widening in wonder.

Before them lay a sparkling waterfall, its crystalline waters cascading down a moss-covered rockface into a clear, tranquil pool. The mist from the falls created a veil of shimmering droplets, casting rainbows in the air. And there, at the water's edge, was a picnic spread, complete with various delectable faerie delicacies.

"Lorien," Elara breathed, turning to him with a look of awe. "This is... it's magical."

Lorien smiled, his eyes holding a warmth that made Elara's heart skip a beat. "I wanted to do something special for you," he said, his voice low and sincere. "To apologize for not being more considerate of what this ordeal must be like for you. I asked the servants to have it ready." He hesitated momentarily, then added, "And to let you know that I sent word by messenger back to your village to let your father and brother know you're safe."

Elara's eyes filled with tears, overwhelmed by his thoughtfulness. *He did this for me,* she marveled, her heart swelling with gratitude and something deeper, something she wasn't quite ready to name. "Thank you, Lorien," she whispered, her voice thick with emotion. "This means more to me than you know."

As they settled onto the picnic blanket, their shoulders brushing, their laughter mingling with the sound of the waterfall, Elara couldn't help but think that, despite the strange circumstances that had brought them together, there was nowhere else she'd rather be.

Perhaps being bound to a faerie prince isn't the worst fate a human girl could suffer, she thought, sneaking a glance at Lorien as he poured her a glass of sparkling faerie wine.

As they ate, Elara sneaked glances at Lorien, her eyes tracing the luminescent markings that danced across his skin. *He's beautiful*, she thought, a blush rising to her cheeks as she quickly looked away, hoping he hadn't noticed her staring.

But Lorien had noticed and found himself equally entranced by the human girl beside him. The way her dark hair cascaded over her shoulders and her eyes sparkled with laughter and curiosity was like nothing he'd ever seen before. *She's so full of life*, he marveled. *So different from the reserved and aloof fairies I've experienced all my life.*

Their eyes met over the rim of their glasses, and the world fell away for a moment. Elara's breath caught in her throat as Lorien leaned in, his hand brushing against hers as he reached for a piece of fruit. The air between them crackled with tension and the unspoken attraction building since they'd first met.

Is he going to kiss me? Elara wondered, her heart racing as Lorien's face drew closer to hers. His breath ghosted across her lips and she searched his green eyes for flecks of gold she'd noticed. For a moment, she forgot about the binding spell and the differences between their worlds. All that mattered was the faerie prince in front of her and the way he made her feel.

But just as their lips were about to touch, Lorien pulled away, his eyes filled with longing and regret. "I'm sorry," he murmured, his voice rough with emotion. "I shouldn't have... I'm just trying to do the right thing."

Elara's heart sank, but she forced a smile to hide the disappointment that washed over her. "Of course," she said, her voice falsely bright. "I understand."

They finished their meal silently, the earlier playfulness replaced by a heavy tension. But even as they avoided each other's gaze, Elara sensed the pull of the binding spell, the way it drew them closer together with each passing moment.

As they packed up the remnants of their picnic, laughter and music drifted through the trees, catching Elara's attention. Curious, she followed the melody, Lorien trailing close behind her. The binding spell did not allow them to stray too far apart.

They stumbled upon a clearing where a group of fairies, including many of Lorien's friends, were practicing dance moves for an upcoming festival. The fairies twirled and leaped, their movements fluid and graceful, their luminescent wings shimmered in the dappled sunlight that filtered through the forest canopy.

Elara gazed in awe as the fairies moved in perfect synchronicity, their laughter and chatter mingling with the music. She turned to Lorien, her eyes wide with wonder. "What's this all about?" she asked, her earlier disappointment forgotten.

Lorien smiled with pride in his voice as he explained, "It's the Faerie Festival of Light, a celebration of the summer solstice. It's essentially the fairies' version of the festival your village will soon have."

Elara's face lit up with excitement. "It's beautiful," she breathed, her gaze returning to the dancing fairies. "Can we join them?"

Lorien hesitated, a flicker of uncertainty crossing his features. But as he looked at Elara, her eyes shining with pure joy and enthusiasm, he found himself unable to resist. "I suppose a little dancing couldn't hurt," he relented, a grin tugging at the corners of his mouth.

Hand in hand, they stepped into the clearing, the binding spell allowing them just enough distance to twirl and spin with the other fairies. Elara let the music wash over her, her body moving naturally to the rhythm, her laughter ringing through the forest as she danced alongside Lorien and his friends.

For a moment, all the worries and tensions were replaced by the sheer exhilaration of the dance. But as they moved together, their bodies drawing closer with each step, Elara couldn't help but notice the way Lorien's gaze lingered on her, and his touch lingered just a fraction longer than necessary.

It's just the spell, she reminded herself, even as her heart raced at his proximity. *It doesn't mean anything.*

But before she could dwell on it further, a familiar voice cut through the music, sharp and accusatory. "Elara, may I have a word with you?"

Aria stood at the edge of the clearing, her ice-blue eyes narrowed as she took in the sight of Elara and Lorien dancing together. Her usually serene expression was marred by a flicker of jealousy, her hands clenched at her sides.

Elara glanced at Lorien, who shrugged helplessly, the binding spell preventing him from straying too far. With a sigh, she followed Aria to a secluded spot outside the clearing, bracing herself for the confrontation she saw coming.

"What exactly is going on between you and Lorien?" Aria demanded, her voice tight with barely contained anger. "You two seem awfully close for a faerie prince and a human girl who just met."

Elara held up her hands in a placating gesture, trying to defuse the situation. "Aria, I promise nothing is going on between us. We're just... we're bound together by this spell, remember? We don't have a choice but to be close."

But even as the words left her mouth, Elara couldn't help but sense a twinge of guilt. While it was true that the binding spell kept her and Lorien in close proximity, she understood that the growing connection between them was more than just magic. It was in the way they laughed together, the way they found comfort in each other's presence, the way their gazes seemed to linger just a little too long to be purely platonic.

Aria, however, was unconvinced. She crossed her arms, her gaze still sharp with suspicion. "I've seen how he looks at you," she said, her voice low and accusing. "The way you two dance together, you're always whispering and laughing. You may be bound by magic, but there's more to it than that."

Elara sighed, running a hand through her hair in frustration. "Aria, I swear to you, Lorien and I are just...friends? Yes, we've grown closer because of this ordeal, but that's all. Friendship."

Even as she spoke the words, Elara couldn't help but wonder if she was trying to convince Aria or herself. Because deep down, in a part of her heart, she wasn't quite ready to acknowledge, she knew that her feelings for Lorien were changing. That the spark between them was more than just the result of a magical binding.

But she couldn't admit that, not to Aria or herself. So instead, she forced a smile, her tone light and joking as she said, "Besides, can you imagine? A human and a faerie prince? It's ridiculous."

Aria's expression relaxed, but the suspicion didn't completely leave her eyes. "I suppose you're right," she said, her tone still guarded. "Just be careful, Elara. Lorien is a prince of the faerie realm. He has duties and obligations that go beyond whatever this... this *thing* is between you two."

With that, she turned and walked away, leaving Elara alone with her thoughts. She glanced back toward the clearing, where Lorien was still dancing with his friends, his laughter carrying on the breeze. Her heart ached at the sight of him, realizing how much he had come to mean to her in such a short time.

Aria's right, she thought, a bitter smile tugging at her lips. *A human and a faerie prince... it could never work. No matter how much I might want it to.*

As Elara approached the group, a thin fae with dark hair and eyes, a deep shade of violet, approached from the other direction. His name was Thorne, and Elara had met him earlier that day at one of the several meetings she'd been dragged to. She'd learned very shortly that the idea that all fairies were beautiful creatures, smaller than humans with wings like butterfly rainbows, was a lie. Faes came in as many varieties as humans. While Lorien was handsome, with silver markings and a muscular frame, Thorne was dark, wiry, and mean-looking. And while he hadn't opened his wings, she could tell they would be thick, dark, and scaly.

Thorne's voice cut through the air like a knife, drawing Elara's attention back to the present. "Lorien, a word?"

Lorien's laughter faded as he turned to face Thorne, his expression guarded. "Of course, Thorne. What is it?"

Thorne's eyes flicked to Elara, a sneer curling his lip. "Perhaps we should speak privately. I wouldn't want to bore your... guest with matters of the court."

Elara felt her cheeks burn at the disdain in Thorne's voice, but Lorien stepped forward his tone firm. "Anything you have to say to me, you can say in front of Elara."

Thorne's eyes narrowed, but he inclined his head in a mockery of respect. "As you wish, Your Highness." He took a step closer, his voice lowering to a hiss. "I've been hearing rumors, Lorien. Whispers about you and this... *human*. People are starting to talk."

Lorien's jaw clenched, his eyes flashing with anger. "And what exactly are they saying, Thorne?"

"That you've grown too close to her. That you're letting your feelings for a mortal cloud your judgment." Thorne's gaze slid back to Elara, a cruel smile twisting his lips. "That you've forgotten your duty to your people in favor of pursuing a forbidden love."

Elara's heart stopped, her breath catching in her throat. *Forbidden love?* Is that what people thought this was?

But Lorien's voice was cold as he replied, "You overstep, Thorne. My relationship with Elara is none of your concern."

"It is when it threatens the stability of our kingdom!" Thorne snapped, his composure slipping for a moment. "You are the prince, Lorien. You have a responsibility to your people and your bloodline. You cannot let yourself be swayed by some... some *subspecies*."

The word hit Elara like a physical blow, and her eyes widened in shock and pain. She sees Lorien stiffen, his hands clenching into fists at his sides.

"You will not speak of her that way," he said, his voice low and dangerous. "Elara is a guest in our kingdom and will be treated with respect."

Thorne scoffed, shaking his head. "You're a fool, Lorien. You're letting your emotions cloud your judgment, which will be your downfall. Galivanting around with her like she's your pet when you should be trying to figure out how to get rid of her."

With that, he turned on his heel and stalked away, leaving a stunned silence in his wake.

Elara realized the eyes of the other fairies were on her, the weight of their judgment and scorn pressing down on her like a physical force. She wanted to run, to hide, to escape the humiliation and pain that Thorne's words had brought.

But then there was a tug on her wrist, a reminder of the binding spell that held her to Lorien. She glanced down, realizing with a start that they were now standing mere inches apart, the spell pulling them closer in response to her distress.

No, she thought, a sudden determination filling her. *I won't let him see how much his words hurt me. I won't give him the satisfaction.*

Taking a deep breath, Elara stepped back from Lorien, a forced smile on her face. "Well," she said, her tone falsely bright. "That was certainly an interesting conversation."

Lorien's brow furrowed, concern etched in every line of his face. "Elara, I'm so sorry. Thorne had no right to say those things to you."

But Elara just shook her head, her smile never wavering. "It's fine, Lorien. Really. I'm used to people underestimating me."

And then, before he could respond, she turned to face the other fairies, her chin held high. "In fact," she said, her voice ringing out clear and strong, "I think it's time I showed you all what a *subspecies* can do."

With that, she took up one of the flutes on the side and stepped into the center of the clearing, her feet moving in time to a beat only she could hear. She let the music fill her, her body swaying and twirling in a dance that was all her own. As if in support, the forest began to echo her music—the wind, the birds, the distant water running through a brook, the scamper of the animal's feet.

She could see the fairies' eyes on her and hear their murmurs of surprise and confusion. But she didn't let it phase her. She lost herself in the rhythm and movement, letting her talent speak for itself.

As she played, she spun and leaped, her dark hair flying out behind her. She caught a glimpse of Lorien's face. His eyes were wide, and his lips parted in wonder as she danced, captivated by the sight of her.

In that moment, Elara experienced a thrill of triumph, a surge of pride and satisfaction that had nothing to do with the binding spell. They did not know her. She could make music. It coursed through her like magic coursed through them. It was her magic.

Some humans, very few, could learn a kind of magic that is connected to something. Elara's mother could, and it was tied to music. The forest was showing the faries what she already knew. She was also one of the few. Untrained, true. But blessed, none the less.

Let them stare, she thought, a pride welling inside. *Let them see what I'm capable of. Let them see what we humans can do.*

Her impromptu performance came to an end as she struck her final pose, the last note issuing from the flute. Breathless and exhilarated, she knew that she had proven herself—not just to the fairies but to herself.

She was Elara Mariposa Santiago, and she was no one's subspecies.

As the final notes of Elara's dance faded, a hush fell over the gathering. Elara, still caught in the exhilaration of her performance, hardly observing she and Lorien drifted apart, the invisible tether between them stretching to nearly six feet.

It was Aria who broke the silence, her voice laced with a hint of bitterness. "Well, well," she said, her ice-blue eyes flicking between Elara and Lorien. "It seems our prince must have some rather positive feelings about his human companion's performance. How else to explain the sudden space between them?"

A flush crept up Elara's neck, but Thorne's mocking laughter cut through the air before she could respond.

"Indeed," he said, his violet eyes glinting with malice. "Quite the provocative display, wasn't it? One might almost think our dear prince was smitten."

Lorien stiffened, his hands clenching into fists at his sides. "Watch your tongue, Thorne," he growled, stepping forward.

But Elara, sensing the rising tension, placed a calming hand on his arm. "It's not worth it," she murmured, meeting his gaze with a steady look. "Let it go."

Aria, too, appeared to recognize the danger of the moment. She moved to Lorien's other side, her voice soft but firm. "She's right, Lorien. Don't let him bait you."

For a moment, Lorien wavered, torn between his anger and the counsel of the two women. But finally, with a visible effort, he relaxed his stance, the fire in his eyes dimming to a smolder.

Thorne, however, was not so easily deterred. As he turned to walk away, his parting shot hung in the air like a poisoned dart. "A prince of fairies, willing to fight over a human woman? Perhaps it's time to reconsider your priorities, Your Highness."

Elara flinched at the words, sensing their sting even as Thorne disappeared into the crowd. *Is that what they all think?* she wondered, her earlier triumph fading into uncertainty. *That I'm just a distraction, a weakness for Lorien to overcome?*

But as she glanced at Lorien and saw his jaw clenched with suppressed anger, she pushed the thought aside. Whatever the others might think, she realized the truth of her own heart. And right now, that truth told her it was time to go.

"Come on," she said, tugging at Lorien's arm. "Let's get out of here."

Lorien hesitated momentarily, his eyes still fixed on where Thorne had disappeared. But then, with a sigh, he nodded, allowing Elara to lead him away from the gathering and into the quiet forest beyond.

One step at a time, Elara told herself as they walked, imagining the invisible bond between them shimmering in the dappled sunlight. *We'll figure this out together.*

As they walked, Lorien's anger dissipated, replaced by a pensive expression. He turned to Elara, his eyes softening. "I apologize for Thorne's behavior. He had no right to speak that way."

Elara shook her head, a wry smile playing at the corners of her mouth. "It's not your fault. I get the idea he's not exactly my biggest fan."

Lorien chuckled, the sound a welcome break in the tension. "No, I suppose not. But still, I should have done more to defend you."

"You did plenty," Elara assured him, remembering how he had stepped forward, ready to take on Thorne for her sake. "But maybe next time, we should just avoid the drama altogether. What do you say we head back to the castle?"

Lorien's eyes lit up at the suggestion. "Of course. And I can fly us there in no time."

Elara's steps faltered, her cheeks warming at the memory of their last flight together, the way her body had molded against his, the electric thrill of his touch. *No*, she thought, *I can't handle that again. Not now, when everything feels so complicated.*

"Actually," she said, her voice higher than usual, "I think I'd rather walk. It's such a beautiful evening, and I could use the exercise."

Lorien's brow furrowed, but he didn't argue. "As you wish. Though I must say, you're missing out on quite the view."

Oh, I don't think I'm missing out on anything, Elara thought, her gaze drifting to the strong lines of his profile and the way the light danced in his silver hair. *The view from down here is pretty spectacular, too.*

But she kept that thought to herself, focusing instead on the path ahead, on putting one foot in front of the other. *One step at a time*, she reminded herself, *one step at a time.*

As they walked, the sun began to dip below the horizon, painting the sky in vibrant hues of orange and pink. Elara couldn't help but gasp at the beauty of it all, the way the colors danced across the clouds.

Lorien glanced at her, a soft smile playing at the corners of his lips. "It's quite something, isn't it? The sunsets in the faerie realm are always spectacular. I've seen them so often that I might take them for granted. But it's wonderful to watch someone new appreciate them as much as you."

Elara's heart skipped a beat at his words and the warmth in his gaze. She opened her mouth to respond, but before she could, a loud crack of thunder echoed through the forest, making her jump.

Lorien's eyes widened. "We need to find shelter quickly. There's a storm coming."

No sooner had he spoken than the sky opened up, rain pouring down in heavy sheets. Elara yelped, throwing her hands up to shield her face from the onslaught. Lorien grabbed her hand, tugging her towards a large tree with sprawling branches that offered some protection from the downpour.

They huddled beneath the leaves, their laughter mingling with the sound of the rain. Elara shivered, her dress clinging to her skin, but she couldn't bring herself to care. Not when Lorien was so close, his body warm and solid against hers.

"Well," she said, grinning at him, "this is certainly an adventure."

Lorien chuckled, brushing a strand of wet hair from her face. "That it is. Though I must say, I'm glad to share it with you."

Elara's breath caught in her throat at the tenderness in his touch and his words' sincerity. *Is this really happening?* she wondered, her heart racing. *Is he feeling this too?*

But before she could dwell on it further, Lorien's expression shifted, his brows knitting together. "Elara, I'm sorry about what happened earlier with Thorne. I shouldn't have let him get to me like that. It's just... he has a way of knowing how to anger me."

Elara reached out, placing a hand on his arm. "It's okay. I understand. I guess things are happening in your world I'm not aware of."

Lorien made a face but didn't attempt to give her any information. She added, "And I think you handled it well for what it's worth. You didn't let him bait you into a fight."

Lorien's lips quirked up in a rueful smile. "Thanks to you. Who knows what might have happened if you hadn't been there to calm me down."

Elara's cheeks warmed at the praise, a pleasant flutter in her stomach. *He's right*, she realized, *I did help him. And not just with Thorne, but with everything. Maybe I'm not as useless as I thought.*

The rain began to slow, fading to a gentle drizzle. Lorien peered out from beneath the branches, his expression thoughtful. "We should probably get going. I don't want you to get cold in those wet clothes."

Elara nodded, stepping out from under the tree. But before she could take more than a few steps, Lorien swept her up into his arms, cradling her against his chest. She let out a surprised squeak, her hands wrapping around his neck.

"Lorien, what are you doing?"

He grinned down at her, his eyes sparkling with mischief. "Flying us back to the castle, of course. I can't have you ruining your beautiful dress by walking through the mud."

Elara's heart raced at the feeling of his strong arms around her. Her eyes fell to the wet shirt that clung to his chest muscles. *This is a bad idea*, she thought, even as she tightened her grip around his neck. *A very, very bad idea.*

But as Lorien took to the sky, the ground falling beneath them, Elara forgot all about her reservations. The sensation of flying was just as exhilarating as she remembered, the rush of the wind and her body's weightlessness. And with Lorien's arms around her, his warmth seeping into her skin, she was safer than ever.

Maybe this isn't such a bad idea after all, she thought, resting her head against his shoulder. *Maybe this is exactly where I'm meant to be.*

As they soared over the forest, the castle rising up in the distance, Elara couldn't help but marvel at the turn her life had taken. Just a few days ago, she had been a simple village girl, dreaming of a life beyond the confines of her small world. And now, here she was, flying through the faerie realm in the arms of a prince, her heart full of possibilities.

I don't know what the future holds, she thought, gazing up at Lorien's profile and the way the moonlight illuminated his features. *But whatever it is, I'm ready for it. Ready for anything, as long as I have him by my side.*

And with that thought, she let herself relax fully into his embrace, savoring the warmth of his body, the strength of his arms. *A girl could get used to this.*

Chapter 7

ELARA SAT CROSS-LEGGED on a cushion in the back of the grand chamber, her eyes wide with wonder as she took in the ethereal beauty of the faerie council room. It was bathed in a soft, golden light that appeared to emanate from the very walls themselves, casting a warm glow on the gathered fairies. Their iridescent wings fluttered delicately, catching the light and creating a kaleidoscope of colors that danced across the room.

Elara recognized the regal Queen among the assembled fairies, resplendent in her flowing gown woven from moonbeams and starlight. Beside her sat Thorne, his angular features sharp and calculating, and Taliesin, his midnight blue hair shimmering as he leaned forward to whisper something in the Queen's ear.

As Elara listened, her brow furrowed with concern as snippets of the fairies' conversation reached her ears. She'd let her mind drift during the meeting the day prior, but the tone of their voices and topics today made her take note. Talk of tensions rising, of armies gathering at the borders, of the looming specter of war.

"They grow bolder with each passing day," Thorne said, his violet eyes flashing. "They encroach upon our lands, their iron weapons poisoning the very earth."

"And what would you have us do, Thorne?" the Queen asked, her voice calm and measured. "Meet their aggression with our own? Plunge our realm into the chaos of war?"

Elara's heart raced as she listened, her mind whirling with the implications of their words. *War? Against the humans?* The very thought made her stomach churn with dread.

She couldn't help but feel a sense of responsibility, a need to bridge the gap between their worlds. Surely there must be a way to foster understanding, to find a path to peace.

As the fairies continued their debate, Elara's gaze drifted to Lorien, who sat silent and pensive, his green eyes distant. She wondered what thoughts weighed on his mind, what burdens he carried as a leader of his people.

Despite the gravity of the situation, Elara couldn't help but get a flutter of excitement at being here, at witnessing this glimpse into the inner workings of the faerie realm. It was a world so different from her own, yet one that called to her with its magic and mystery.

Lorien finally spoke, his voice resonating with quiet authority. "The situation is under control. Our scouts are monitoring the Orc activity closely, and our enchantments protect the heart of our realm."

Orcs? Elara scooted herself closer. So it wasn't the humans that they were fighting with. But there weren't any Orcs in the entire kingdom. Elara's village was sandwiched between the forest, which was part of the Faerie Realm, and the human kingdom her village was part of. She had no idea what was beyond.

Lorien met the Queen's gaze, his expression resolute. "We must not let fear guide our actions. Our strength lies in our unity, in our connection to the land and to each other."

Thorne scoffed, his features twisting into a sneer. "Unity? How can we speak of unity when our prince's attention is divided? He seems to be united to something else currently."

Elara tensed, a chill running down her spine. *Divided attention? What does he mean?*

Lorien's eyes narrowed, his posture stiffening. "Speak plainly, Thorne. What are you implying?"

"I'm merely pointing out the obvious," Thorne replied, his tone dripping with disdain. "Your fascination with the human girl is a distraction, a weakness that our enemies could exploit. We have a war looming against one enemy while our Prince is tethered to another."

Elara's breath caught in her throat, her cheeks burning with a mix of embarrassment and indignation. *Is that how they see me? As a distraction, a liability?*

She fought the urge to shrink back, to hide from the weight of their scrutiny. A few of the council members looked back at her. She was sitting in a chair as far away from the table as the enchantment would allow her—yet somehow, at this moment, it wasn't far enough. She straightened her spine, determined not to show that their judgemental eyes felt like hot coals.

Lorien's voice was low and dangerous, his green eyes flashing with contained anger. "You overstep, Thorne. My personal affairs are none of your concern. Besides, it is known by the counsel she is bound to me magically. Her presence here isn't a *choice.* "

The air in the room crackled with unspoken animosity. Elara's heart raced, her mind whirling with the implications of Thorne's words.

Could my presence here really be putting them at risk? Am I a distraction, pulling Lorien's focus from his duties?

The Queen's melodic voice cut through the tension, drawing all eyes to her. "Enough of this bickering," she said, her tone firm yet gentle. "We have more pressing matters to discuss, such as the upcoming Festival of Light. A Festival to lighten the soul and make the magic churn stronger is exactly what we need."

She rose from her throne, her iridescent wings fluttering behind her. "The festival is a time for joy, for celebration. It is a reminder of the beauty and wonder that still exists in our world, even in the face of darkness. And it's part of strengthing our connection to this land. And this land gives us strength to protect ourselves."

Elara was grateful for the Queen, relieved that the focus had shifted away from her. She observed the other fairies murmur in agreement, their expressions softening at the mention of the festival.

"I have been overseeing the preparations myself," the Queen continued, a smile playing at the corners of her lips. "And I must say, this year's festival promises to be the most spectacular yet. Our people need something positive to look forward too."

She gestured to a slender faerie with gossamer wings, who stepped forward with a bow. "Aria, tell us about the enchanted lanterns you've been crafting."

Aria's eyes sparkled with excitement as she spoke. "We've been infusing the lanterns with starlight and moonbeams, Your Majesty. When released, they will dance across the night sky, painting it with shimmering hues of silver and gold."

Elara's heart swelled with anticipation, her imagination conjuring images of the breathtaking display. *How magical it must be, to witness such beauty firsthand.*

She wondered if she'd be here to see it, or if the spell would just disappear as quickly as it had appeared, and she'd find herself banished back to her village.

The Queen nodded approvingly, then turned to a burly faerie with a crown of leaves adorning his brow. "And what of the music, Oakley? Have you composed something unforgettable?"

Oakley grinned, his deep voice resonating through the chamber. "Indeed, Your Majesty. The melodies will weave through the air like a gentle breeze, filling the hearts of all who hear them with pure, unbridled joy."

Elara closed her eyes for a moment, almost able to hear the enchanting strains of faerie music in her mind. *What I wouldn't give to be a part of such a celebration, to lose myself in the magic and wonder of it all.*

As the fairies continued to share their contributions, each more marvelous than the last, Elara's earlier unease begin to dissipate. The festival sounded like a true spectacle.

Perhaps this is exactly what we need, she mused, sneaking a glance at Lorien. *A chance to come together, to forget our troubles and differences, even if only for a night.*

The Queen's melodic voice cut through Elara's musings, drawing all eyes to her. "I hear Lorien and our charming guest, Elara, participated in the performance rehearsals yesterday. Quite the exhibition, from what I've been told."

Heat rose to her cheeks as the fairies turned to regard her with a mix of curiosity and surprise. She met Lorien's gaze, seeing her uncertainty reflected in his eyes.

"Indeed, Your Majesty," Lorien replied, his tone carefully neutral. "Elara's musical talents are quite remarkable."

The Queen smiled, a glint of mischief in her eyes. "Then perhaps you two would honor us with a duet at the festival? It would be a wonderful way to showcase the unity between our realms."

Elara's heart skipped a beat, a rush of excitement and trepidation flooding through her. *A duet? With Lorien?* The thought was both thrilling and terrifying.

Lorien, too, appeared hesitant, his brow furrowed as he considered his mother's request. Elara could almost see the gears turning in his mind, weighing the implications of such a performance.

What would it mean for us? she wondered, her fingers unconsciously tapping out a nervous rhythm on her thigh. *Would it bring us closer together or only serve to highlight the chasm between us?*

As the silence stretched on, Elara's heart raced, her mind whirling with the possibilities and the potential consequences.

But isn't this what I've always wanted? a small voice whispered in her mind. *A chance to share my music, to connect with others through the power of song?*

She glanced at Lorien again, seeing the conflict in his eyes, the way his hand tightened almost imperceptibly on the arm of his chair.

Suddenly a shimmering light enveloped Elara's chair, and with a gentle tug, it slid across the floor, coming to rest right beside Lorien's. Elara let out a surprised gasp, her eyes widening as she found herself mere inches from the faerie prince.

Lorien was taken aback, his piercing gaze locking with hers as a flicker of amusement danced in their depths. The corners of his lips twitched as if fighting back a smile, and Elara couldn't help but mirror his expression.

The Queen's laughter rang out, a melodic sound that filled the room with warmth and joy. "It seems even the magic of our realm is eager for this duet," she said, her eyes twinkling with mirth.

Elara blushed, the unexpected proximity to Lorien sending a flutter through her stomach. She sensed the heat of his body, the faint scent of blooming flowers and crisp autumn leaves that clung to his skin. She wanted to reach out and cover his hand with hers, but she remembered Thorne's eagle eyes were on them. Instead, she just smiled.

Is this what it would be like, she wondered, *to be so close to him, to share the stage and pour our hearts into a single song?*

The thought was both exhilarating and daunting, a mix of anticipation and nerves that set her pulse racing. She glanced at Lorien again, seeing the same mix of emotions reflected in his eyes.

"Well," he said, his voice a low murmur that sent a shiver down her spine, "it seems we have little choice in the matter."

Elara swallowed hard, her mouth suddenly dry as she nodded in agreement. "I suppose we don't," she whispered, a small, tentative smile tugging at her lips.

The Queen clapped her hands, drawing their attention back to the rest of the room. "Then it's settled," she declared, her voice ringing with authority and delight. "Lorien and Elara will perform a duet at the Festival of Light, a symbol of the unity and harmony between our worlds."

As the other fairies murmured, some with approval, others in confusion, Elara felt a swell of excitement and determination rising within her.

This is my chance to prove that music has the power to bring us all together—to bridge the gap between our realms.

She glanced at Lorien once more, seeing the same determination in his eyes, tempered by a hint of uncertainty.

"You're majesty," Thorne began, just a bit too much honey dripping in his voice, "is that wise? We already have the Orc situation to deal with. Now you want to focus on bridging a gap with a species—"

"Humans," Elara injected. Thorne shot her a withering look.

"—when were already stretched thin?" he finished.

The Queen turned toward Thorne. Elara could swear she saw him shrink back. It was obvious the Queen was not someone anyone wanted to cross.

"Stretched thin, yes. And imagine if the humans continue to encroach on our border on their side? Imagine if they came in here looking to *rescue* Elara from the vile Fairies that kidnapped her, and we had to deal with that on top of the Orc problem? What if we had to divert magic to deal with that problem? Would it not be better to make friends with those who could become enemies? Those who one day may face the same enemy as us and may need to become allies?"

She walked around the council table, making eye contact with each council member in attendance. Elara could see she was quite the motivator.

"Maybe this spell that chose to bind my son and this human was the forest's way of helping us. Telling us that the time to put differences aside is now. Reminding us we have more in common than we think—and as neighbors, we might need to rely on those commonalities."

She stopped behind Thorne's chair, placing a graceful, yet somehow dangerous looking, hand on the chair behind him.

"No, I think the spell is a good thing. I think the duet is a way to show the whole population that a bond and alliance with humans is to our benefit."

The council began to mummer again, this time all in agreement, save Thorne, who looked very annoyed.

"Yes, and I want to see Elara dance again!" Taliesin said, eyes sparkling. He gave her a wink, and she giggled. Lorien just rolled his eyes. And Elara had a twinge of joy that she hadn't experienced in a long time.

Chapter 8

THE SANTIAGO HOUSEHOLD bustled with frantic energy as Hector, Dante, and Cassia gathered supplies for the search party. Worry etched deep lines into Hector's face as he stuffed a pack with rope, torches, and a small hatchet.

"We need to cover more ground," he said gruffly. "Dante, you take the northern path. Cassia, you're with me heading south."

Cassia nodded, her dark curls bouncing. She grabbed a water skin and extra blankets. "What about the eastern woods? That's where she loves to explore."

Hector's jaw clenched. "No. We're not going anywhere near those cursed trees. Elara knows better than to venture there."

Dante opened his mouth to protest, but Hector's sharp look silenced him. He shouldered his pack, worry for his sister was warring with the desire to respect his father's orders.

Just then, a knock sounded at the door. Hector yanked it open to reveal a striking figure - luminescent markings traced his skin and silver hair fell in a metallic sheen. Unmistakably fae.

Hector's eyes narrowed. "What business do you have here?" His voice was sharp with restrained anger.

The messenger bowed his head slightly. "I come bearing a message from Lord Lorien Everoak. He wishes to speak with you regarding your daughter's disappearance."

"Elara is missing and you dare show your face here?" Hector seethed, his knuckles white as he gripped the door frame. "Your kind have done enough damage to my family. Leave, before I do something I regret."

The messenger stood his ground, green eyes flashing. "I understand your distress, but I assure you, we mean no harm. Lord Lorien only wants to help."

Hector looked ready to physically remove the faerie from his doorstep, years of resentment and grief boiling to the surface. In his mind, the fae were responsible for taking away his beloved wife. And now, with Elara missing, those old wounds ripped open anew, leaving him raw and desperate to lash out at the beings he held responsible for so much pain.

Cassia stepped forward, placing a calming hand on Hector's shoulder. "Let's hear what the messenger has to say, Hector. We need all the help we can get to find Elara."

Hector shrugged off her touch, his glare never leaving the fairy's face. "I don't need the help of the likes of him. They've brought nothing but misery to us."

The messenger's expression remained composed, though a flicker of frustration crossed his features. "I apologize for any distress our presence may cause, but I implore you to consider reading Lord Lorien's message."

The fae extended a scroll. Hector just looked down at it, but Casses accepted it with a smile.

"Thank you, kind sir."

The messenger rustled his wings in agitation. Cassia seized the opportunity, moving to stand between Hector and the messenger. "We appreciate your willingness to assist us," she said, her tone even and diplomatic. "Please convey our gratitude to Lord Everoak."

Hector rounded on Cassia. "We don't need their help," he growled, his face flushed with anger. "I won't have those creatures meddling in our affairs."

Cassia met his gaze steadily, her voice firm but gentle. "Hector, I know your distrust runs deep, but we must think of Elara. If the fairies can help us find her, we should at least hear what they have to say."

Hector paced the room, his hands clenching and unclenching at his sides. The thought of accepting anything from the very beings he blamed for his wife's death grated against every fiber of his being. But beneath the anger, fear for his daughter's safety gnawed at him. If there was even a chance the fairies could help bring Elara home...

He sighed heavily, the fight draining from his posture. "Fine, Cassia. We'll hear the *Lord Everoak's* words. But I make no promises."

Cassia nodded, a glimmer of hope in her eyes. "That's all I ask, Hector."

Cassia unrolled the scroll. It was a brief message and didn't make much sense to most of those listening to its reading, though Cassia knew a little of magic and understood a bit.

"So he's kidnapped my girl and taken her back to his palace," Hector said, snatching the paper.

"That's not exactly what it says—"

"First, they took my wife, now my daughter!"

A general ripple of anger from fellow villagers filled the room. They all knew the story.

The messenger shifted uneasily as the anger in the room swelled. He had delivered Lord Lorien's message as instructed, but the humans' reaction was far from the understanding and cooperation he had hoped for.

The faerie inclined his head, a glimmer of ice in his eyes. He could think of about twelve spells to incinerate all the humans in the room. But it wouldn't even be necessary. Bare hands would do.

Instead of retorting, he remembered his mission. "Thank you for your consideration. I shall await your response. Whenever you're ready meet me at the edge of the woods, and I'll take your response back, or perhaps a few items to make her more comfortable during her stay."

"Her *stay?*" Hector mocked. "Her kidnapping you mean!"

Turning to Cassia, the messenger bowed deeply. "Thank you for your kindness, my lady. It is rare to find a human with such an open mind and gentle heart."

Cassia smiled warmly. "I only wish for peace and understanding between our peoples. I hope that one day, we can move past this distrust and find a way to coexist harmoniously."

The messenger's eyes flickered to Hector and the other villagers, their hostility evident. "I fear that day may be far off, but your words give me hope." He glanced towards the door, eager to depart before the situation escalated. "I'll wait until the sun begins to set near the edge of the forest. Come whenever you are ready. I pray that you find young Elara safe and sound when she returns."

With a final nod to Cassia, the messenger swiftly exited the house, his iridescent wings catching the light as he took to the sky. As he flew over the village, he couldn't shake the unease in his heart. The humans' fear and ignorance were a dangerous combination, and he worried about the consequences of their misguided actions.

No sooner had the faerie messenger disappeared than the villagers erupted into a frenzy of anger and fear.

"They've taken Elara!"

"Those wretched fairies, always stealing our loved ones!"

"We can't let them get away with this!"

The crowd surged forward, their voices rising in a cacophony of fury. Hector, his face twisted with rage, grabbed a torch from the wall. "We'll make them pay for what they've done. We'll burn their precious forest to the ground to bring her back if we have to!"

The villagers roared their approval, arming themselves with torches, pitchforks, and any makeshift weapons they could find.

Cassia looked on in horror as the mob whipped into a frenzy. She listened to ideas turn to plans of destruction and violence.

"No, stop!" Cassia cried over their voices. "You don't understand! This isn't the way!" But no one was listening as her pleas were drowned out by their anger.

I fear what this misunderstanding will bring, Cassia thought, her heart heavy with dread. *If only they could see that violence and hatred will only breed more of the same. We must find another way before it's too late.*

Hector paced back and forth, his eyes wild with a mixture of anger and fear. "She must have been kidnapped," he insisted, his voice rising with each word. "Those wretched fairies took her, I know it! There is no spell that would make Elara leave us willingly."

Dante shook his head, his brow furrowed with concern. "Father, we don't know that for certain. Elara is strong and capable. Perhaps she had a reason for leaving that we're not aware of."

Hector whirled around, his face contorted with rage. "Reason? What reason could she possibly have for abandoning her family? No, those fairies are behind this, and I won't rest until I have her back!"

Cassia stepped forward, her hands held out in a placating gesture. "Hector, please, let's think this through. Rushing into the forest with anger and accusations will only make matters worse."

Hector scoffed, his eyes narrowing. "And what would you have us do, Cassia? Sit back and wait while those creatures do God knows what to my daughter?"

Cassia took a deep breath, her voice calm and measured. "I suggest we send a small party to the castle to gather more information and try to resolve this misunderstanding peacefully. If we approach them with respect and a willingness to listen, perhaps we can find a solution that benefits everyone."

Dante nodded, his eyes lighting up with hope. "Cassia's right, Father. Elara always spoke of the fairies with such reverence. I can't believe they would harm her. Let's give them a chance to explain before we do something we might regret."

Hector's shoulders sagged, the fight draining out of him as he considered their words.

They're just children, he thought, his heart heavy with worry. *They don't understand the dangers that lurk in those cursed woods.*

He shook his head, his voice gruff as he spoke. "No. I won't risk anyone else falling into their clutches. We'll get Elara out on our own, without the help of those treacherous fairies."

Cassia and Dante exchanged a frustrated glance. As Hector turned away, Cassia leaned in close to Dante, her voice a hushed whisper. "We can't let this continue, Dante. The longer we wait, the more danger Elara could be in."

Dante nodded, his eyes sparkling with mischief. "I have an idea, but we'll need to be quick and quiet." He gestured towards the kitchen, where their packs lay waiting. "We'll gather supplies and sneak out before anyone notices. Once we're in the forest, we can convince that messenger to take us to Elara. We'll bring her home before this misunderstanding turns into an all-out war."

Cassia grinned, her heart swelling with pride at Dante's bravery and resourcefulness. "Let's do it. For Elara."

As the household bustled with activity, Cassia and Dante slipped away, their packs laden with food, water, and other essentials. They moved soundlessly through the village, their eyes scanning the horizon for any sign of trouble.

Hold on, Elara, Dante thought, his jaw set with determination. *We're coming for you.*

Together, they disappeared into the enchanted forest, their hearts filled with hope and a fierce determination to bring Elara home and restore the makeshift truce that existed between themselves and their neighbors.

Chapter 9

ELARA'S FINGERS DANCED across the keys of the harpsichord, her hazel eyes alight with enthusiasm as she played a lively melody. Lorien sat beside her, his brow furrowed as he studied the sheet music spread out before them.

"I think we should choose something more energetic for the duet," Elara said, her voice carrying the same bounce as her music. "Something that will make people want to get up and dance!"

Lorien pursed his lips, his green eyes flickering to meet hers. "I respectfully disagree. A more subdued and elegant composition would be far more fitting for the occasion."

As they debated, Elara sensed the now-familiar tug of the proximity spell pulling them closer together. She tried to shift on the bench to maintain some distance, but the invisible force drew her inexorably towards Lorien.

Oh not again, she thought with a mix of amusement and exasperation. *This spell really has impeccable timing.*

Their shoulders bumped, and then her thigh practically put itself on top of his, throwing off Elara's playing. Lorien reached for his lute at the exact moment, and their hands collided in a tangle of fingers. They both froze, laughter bubbling up at the absurdity of the situation.

"Well, I suppose we'll have to get used to this," Elara chuckled, trying to ignore the way her heart fluttered at Lorien's touch. She met his gaze, noting the way his stern expression softened with reluctant amusement.

"Indeed," he agreed, a faint smile tugging at the corners of his mouth. "Though I do hope we can resolve our creative differences with more ease than we can escape this spell's pull."

Elara grinned, appreciating his dry wit. Despite their opposing views, she couldn't help but be drawn to Lorien in a way that had nothing to do with magic.

There's more to him than that aloof exterior, she mused, studying the graceful lines of his face, the sparkle of humor in his eyes. *I just need to find a way to reach him.*

Aloud, she said, "I'm open to compromise. Perhaps we could find a middle ground - something with an elegant melody but a lively rhythm underneath. The best of both worlds."

Lorien considered her words, his long fingers absently plucking at the strings of his lute. The sound reverberated through Elara, sending a pleasant shiver down her spine.

"A reasonable suggestion," he acknowledged after a moment. "Shall we experiment with a few options and see what we can create together?"

"I'd like nothing more," Elara beamed, already reaching for her sheet music, her mind awhirl with possibilities.

As they began to play once more, their instruments and bodies brushing with each movement, Elara couldn't help but be excited. She found herself captivated by the way Lorien's fingers danced across the strings of his lute, his movements as graceful and precise as a conductor leading an orchestra. She eyed him, transfixed, her own playing almost an afterthought.

She imagined his fingers strumming across her like that, and quickly shook her head and came back to the moment.

He's so talented, she thought, admiring the way he lost himself in the music, his eyes half-closed, his expression one of pure focus and passion. *If only I could convince him to sing as well...*

An idea sparked in her mind, and before she could second-guess herself, Elara blurted out, "Your mother once told me you have a beautiful singing voice. Your voice is what caused me to come into the forest, after all."

Lorien's fingers faltered on the strings, a discordant note ringing out in the sudden silence. He looked at her, his eyes wide with surprise and a flicker of vulnerability.

"Singing?" he asked, his voice just above a whisper.

Elara nodded, her heart aching at the raw emotion in his tone. "She said it was one of her greatest joys, to hear you sing. That your voice could make even the stars weep with its beauty."

Lorien swallowed hard, his gaze dropping to his lute. "I haven't sung in public," he admitted, his words heavy with grief and longing.

Oh, Lorien... Elara's heart went out to him, and she found herself reaching out to lay a comforting hand on his arm, the spell pulling them closer together.

"I understand," she murmured, her thumb rubbing soothing circles on his skin. "It can be scary... but I think she would want you to sing. To share that gift with the world. Or else why would she tell a babbler mouth like me? She knew I'd bring it up."

Lorien met her gaze, his smile tugging at his lips.

Then, slowly, he nodded. "Alright," he whispered, his voice rough with emotion. "For her. And for you."

Elara's breath caught in her throat, her heart swelling with a mixture of anticipation and affection. She squeezed his arm, offering him a smile of encouragement.

"Whenever you're ready," she said gently, her own instrument forgotten in her lap.

Lorien took a deep breath, his eyes sliding shut. And then, he began to sing.

As Lorien's voice filled the room, Elara found herself captivated by its ethereal beauty. The melody danced in the air, each note imbued with the magic of the Faerie realm. His voice was rich and haunting, conveying a depth of emotion that made her heart ache with longing.

Lost in the enchantment of his song, Elara almost forgot to breathe. She stared at him, transfixed, as the golden light filtering through the windows cast a halo around his silver hair, making him look like a celestial being.

When the last note faded away, Elara blinked, as if waking from a dream. "Lorien," she breathed, her voice filled with awe. "That was... breathtaking."

Lorien opened his eyes, a faint blush coloring his cheeks. "Thank you," he murmured, his gaze meeting hers with an intensity that made her heart skip a beat.

In that moment, Elara dug deep for courage. Singing the songs of others is one thing—sharing your own music was entirely different. She reached for the sheets of music in her pocket. The night after the Queen's duet assignment she'd had some ideas. It was an extension of the song she'd be planning for the human festival. The pages somewhat crumpled from her nervous grip. "I've been working on something," she said, her voice trembling. "A new song. And I... I was hoping you might help me with it."

She held out the pages to him, her heart pounding in her chest. This song was more than just a composition to her; it was a piece of her soul, a reflection of her deepest emotions.

Lorien took the pages, his eyes scanning the notes with curiosity. As he read, his expression softened, a bright smile spreading across his face. "Elara, this is beautiful," he said, his voice filled with admiration.

Warmth rushed over her at his praise. "I was hoping," she whispered, "that with a few faerie instruments and your voice... it could be perfect."

Lorien looked up at her, his green eyes shining with understanding. "I would be honored to help," he said, his hand brushing against hers as he handed the pages back to her.

As their fingers touched, Elara felt a spark of electricity run through her, the spell pulling them closer together. She swallowed hard, her gaze locked with his, the air between them filled with a tension that was both exhilarating and terrifying.

"I was thinking," Lorien said, his voice breaking the silence, "that we could incorporate some of the unique sounds of our instruments. Infuse the song with the magic of our realm."

Elara nodded eagerly, her mind already racing with possibilities. "Yes. That would be perfect."

As they began to work on the song together, Elara's mind drifted to a sense of unity and purpose that she had never experienced before. She loved music, and she knew of the power it had. However, this was the first time she'd ever been part of it so wholly. Their collaboration was a dance of give and take, each contributing their unique talents and perspectives.

And through it all, Elara fell deeper and deeper under the spell of Lorien's presence, the magic of their connection growing stronger with each passing moment.

Elara noted the spell's hold loosening as they continued to work on the duet, allowing them to move further apart. She took a step back, marveling at the progress they had made, both in their music and in their relationship. Lorien's eyes met hers, a smile playing at the corners of his lips.

"I never thought I'd enjoy collaborating with a human so much," he admitted, his voice soft and filled with wonder. "You've opened my eyes to a whole new world of possibilities, Elara."

Elara's heart skipped a beat at his words, a warm blush spreading across her cheeks. "I feel the same way," she confessed, her fingers absentmindedly brushing against his as she reached for her sheet music. "Working with you has been an incredible experience."

Throughout their practice, Elara and Lorien found themselves lost in each other's company, sharing stories and laughter between the notes of their duet. As they worked, their interactions became more comfortable and intimate. Elara made excuses to touch him, her hand lingering on his shoulder as she leaned in to point out a particular passage in the music or her fingers brushing against his as they reached for the same instrument.

Lorien, too, found ways to close the distance between them, his hand resting on the small of her back as he guided her through a tricky section of the composition, or his breath tickling her ear as he leaned in to whisper a suggestion.

As they experimented with different melodies, harmonies, and rhythms, Elara and Lorien seamlessly blended their unique musical styles and cultural influences. Lorien's elegant, ethereal fae compositions intertwined with Elara's lively, passionate human rhythms, creating an enchanting and invigorating duet. The music room filled with the sounds of their collaboration, a fusion of their talents and a celebration of their shared love for music.

Elara closed her eyes, losing herself in the magic of the moment. As they played and sang together, their voices intertwined, creating a harmonious and mesmerizing sound that resonated throughout the room. The air seemed to shimmer with the power of their connection, a tangible energy that wrapped around them like a warm embrace.

"This is incredible. I never fathomed music could be like this."

Lorien's eyes met hers, a deep understanding passing between them. "It's because of us," he said softly, his hand reaching out to brush a stray lock of hair from her face. "Our connection, our emotions... they're pouring into the music, making it something truly special."

Elara leaned into his touch, her heart racing at the intimacy of the gesture. She expected him to pull away, but he didn't. He let a soft thumb lightly rub her cheek, and she leaned more into his palm. She wasn't sure how long she stood there, eyes closed, content to be tethered to a fae she didn't understand. She opened her eyes to see him looking down at her, something new hidden behind his eyes. She sensed the bond loosen a bit, but he didn't move away.

Instead, he leaned in and placed a gentle kiss on her lips. The thrill that filled her started from the edge of her toes and fluttered to the top of her head. She dropped the papers she was holding and snaked an arm around his neck, pulling him into her. A sound, not a groan, more like a hum, came from him as he moved his hand from her face to her rear end and pulled her closer to him.

The kiss felt like it lasted forever. When they broke apart, both breathed heavily and looked confused. Especially Lorien. He stood looking at her as embarrassment caused her to try to busy herself with something, anything. She tried to round the table to pick up the papers that had scattered on the floor, but a hard tug pulled her right back to Lorien, this time her back and bottom flush to him.

"Mother of a freakin' dragon!" she huffed, refusing to turn around.

Lorien simply took the paper from her hand and then began walking around wordlessly, helping her pick up the papers. Anyone who came in would have come upon an amusing sight. The human woman molded into the prince like a perfect song, both walking and bending over together in unison.

And every time they bent over Elara cursed. She could feel Lorien against her backside. She could feel all of him. And while his mouth was quiet, other body parts were speaking volumes.

After they finished, Lorien whispered in her ear. "One more practice? You play, since you're in front. We'll both sing."

As Lorien sang, she could feel the vibration in his chest and his breath on her neck. If she wasn't tethered to him, her knees would buckle, and she'd be on the ground.

She managed to come in on her cues, though a bit off-tone. She was happy she couldn't see Lorien's face.

Once the song finished, he allowed his lips to grace her neck. "Perfect."

He took her hands from the harpsichord and rubbed them in an intimate gesture.

"And since I can't be seen walking around in our current state, I say we adjourned to our room early before we give the servants something to talk about."

Quietly, step-in-step, the two made their way to the room that had been set up to allow at least a foot of space between them. Elara was imagining what the rest of the night would be like, while Lorien wondered why a kiss would have bound them so close instead of allowing for more distance.

Neither had answers. But they both knew one thing: they were definitely sleeping in the same bed that night.

Chapter 10

ELARA SHIFTED UNCOMFORTABLY, her body pressed flush against Lorien's as they stood awkwardly in the middle of the bedchamber. She could feel the heat radiating from his skin, the firmness of his muscles, and the unmistakable evidence of his arousal pressing into her lower back. A blush crept up her neck. She tried to subtly adjust her position to ease the intimate contact, but the magical binding held fast, allowing only the slightest wiggle room.

Lorien drew in a sharp breath at her movement. His hands resting lightly on her waist tensed. He cleared his throat. "My apologies, Lady Elara. I did not intend...That is, I would not presume to..." His usually eloquent words trailed off as he struggled to navigate the unfamiliar territory of their predicament.

Elara's lips quirked into a rueful smile, though he could not see it. Poor Lorien sounded as flustered as she felt. Taking a deep breath, she aimed for a light, teasing tone. "Well, Your Highness, it seems we have quite the dilemma on our hands. Or rather, our entire bodies." She giggled, trying to diffuse the tension. "Since we appear to be rather...stuck...I propose we make the best of it and get some rest. Entirely clothed, of course," she hastened to add.

Lorien huffed out a surprised chuckle at her jest. The sound reverberated through her, warm and rich. "Indeed, my lady. A practical solution." He paused, and she could practically hear the gears turning in his head. "Are you certain you would be comfortable with such an arrangement? I would not want to impose..."

Elara's heart swelled at his concern, even amidst their bizarre circumstances. He was not at all what she expected from a faerie prince. She was never entirely convinced of the monstrous picture her father had painted that all fairies were terrible. Still, she now realized she'd never considered how good and kind they could be. She'd never considered *she could actually like them.*

Mustering her courage, she squeezed his hand resting on her hip. "I appreciate your chivalry, Prince Lorien. But seeing as we're already in quite a compromising position, I think propriety has flown out the window. Sleeping side by side will be no hardship." She bit her lip, then couldn't resist impishly adding, "Unless you snore, of course. Then we may have a problem."

Startled laughter burst from Lorien and she joined in, the shared mirth chasing away the worst of the awkwardness. "I assure you, I have been reliably informed that I do not snore," he said with mock affront. He returned her hand squeeze. "Thank you Elara for making light of this frankly ridiculous situation. Your good humor is a balm in trying times."

Warmth spread across her, and something fluttered deep in her chest. Determinedly ignoring it, she lifted her chin. "Well then, shall we see if we can maneuver ourselves into a halfway comfortable sleeping position? I fear it will be a bit like playing a game of Unknot, but we'll muddle through somehow..."

She could perceive Lorien's smile against her hair as they shuffled awkwardly towards the bed, still locked in their strange embrace. Elara focused on putting one foot in front of the other and vehemently told the butterflies rioting in her stomach to settle down.

They were just two people making the best of an impossible situation. No need to read anything more into it, no matter how soft Lorien's featherlight touches were as he helped ease her down to the mattress, his strong arms cradling her close. Or how his spicy, evergreen scent filled her nose, giving her the sensation of being safe and cherished. Or how the press of his body against the length of hers set her every nerve alight with a yearning she didn't dare name...

She closed her eyes, determined to will herself to sleep. They would get through this night—and the days ahead—with poise and practicality. Even if being this close to Lorien made her want, desperately, to throw caution to the wind, to discover all the mysteries and wonders he hid beneath his calm exterior.

She would be sensible. Rational. Keep her inconvenient feelings locked away.

Ignore her loud traitorous heart that whispered that it was already far, far too late for that.

Elara's mind drifted as she lay in Lorien's bed, hyper-aware of his solid presence behind her, his arm draped over her waist. Through the thin fabric of her dress, she could feel the steady rise and fall of his chest, the warmth of his skin seeping into hers. It was both comforting and maddening, this enforced closeness.

Her thoughts spun in dizzying circles, replaying the events that had led them here. The disastrous first encounter, the ancient binding spell, the way Lorien's eyes had widened in shock and then narrowed in anger when they'd first found themselves stuck together. She'd been so certain then that he despised her, that he saw her as nothing more than an inconvenience, a human interloper in his perfect faerie world.

But then... then there had been moments. Glimmers of connection, of understanding. The way he'd looked at her as they'd danced at the practice for the festival, his gaze intense and searching. The gentleness in his touch as he'd helped her navigate the unfamiliar palace corridors. The vulnerability in his voice when he'd confessed his doubts and fears.

Could it be possible that he was just as confused, just as torn as she was? Could it be that beneath his cool, aloof exterior, he also sensed the pull of something deeper, something that defied the centuries of mistrust and prejudice between their peoples?

Elara's heart raced at the thought, even as her practical side warned her not to get carried away. They were from different worlds, bound by duty and tradition. To imagine anything more was foolish and dangerous even.

And yet... as Lorien shifted, his arm tightening around her waist, Elara couldn't help but wonder. What if, despite all the obstacles and all the reasons that it could never work... what if they were meant to find each other? What if this unexpected, magical bond was a sign, a chance for something extraordinary?

Slowly, hardly daring to breathe, Elara let her hand come to rest over Lorien's where it lay on her stomach. His skin was warm, the muscles firm beneath her tentative touch. He stirred, his breath ghosting over the back of her neck, and she froze, suddenly afraid she'd crossed a line.

But Lorien merely sighed, a soft, contented sound, and nuzzled closer, his nose brushing the sensitive spot behind her ear. Elara's eyes fluttered closed, a shiver running through her that had nothing to do with the cool night air.

Tomorrow, she told herself, even as she laced her fingers through his and let herself sink into his embrace. Tomorrow they would figure this out, find a way to break the spell and go back to their separate lives.

But tonight... tonight, she would allow herself this. This one stolen moment of connection, of possibility. This fragile, fleeting glimpse of what could be if only the world were a different place.

Elara lay perfectly still, her senses heightened to every point of contact between her body and Lorien's. She focused on the rise and fall of his chest against her back and the brush of his exhalations stirring the fine hairs at the nape of her neck. His arm was a comforting weight across her waist, his long fingers splayed over her stomach in a gesture that was both protective and intimate.

Despite the unfamiliar sensation of being held so closely, Elara found herself relaxing into Lorien's embrace. There was a rightness to it, a sense of belonging that she'd never experienced before. It was as though their bodies had been designed to fit together, two puzzle pieces finally slotting into place.

Lost in her musings, Elara almost didn't register when Lorien spoke, his voice a low rumble that vibrated through her. "Elara, I... I want to apologize."

She blinked, turning her head slightly in an attempt to see his face. "Apologize? For what?"

Lorien sighed, his breath ghosting over her cheek. "For the how I treated you when we first met. I was rude and dismissive, and I made assumptions about you based on nothing more than the fact that you're human. It was unfair of me, and I'm sorry."

Elara's heart stuttered in her chest. She'd never expected to hear those words from him, never dared to hope that he might see past the prejudices that had colored their initial interactions. "Thank you," she whispered, her voice thick with emotion. "I know it couldn't have been easy for you to say that."

Lorien's arm tightened around her, drawing her even closer against him. "I'm beginning to realize that there's a lot about humans - about you - that I don't know. But I want to learn. I want to understand."

Elara smiled, a warm glow suffusing her chest. "I'd like that," she murmured, letting her eyes drift closed. "I'd like that very much."

For a long moment, they lay in silence, the only sound the gentle whisper of their breath. Elara was hyperaware of every place their bodies touched, the heat of Lorien's skin seeping through the thin fabric of her dress. It was a strange sort of intimacy, born of circumstance rather than choice, but no less profound.

"Elara," Lorien murmured, his voice barely audible even in the quiet of the room. "There's something else I need to tell you."

He shifted behind her, his muscles tensing as if steeling himself for some great confession. "What is it?" she asked, her heart beginning to race.

"I..." Lorien paused. "I think I'm developing feelings for you," he said at last, the words rushing out of him in a breathless tumble. "Feelings that go beyond mere friendship or alliance. Feelings that I never thought I would have for a human."

Elara's breath caught in her throat, her mind reeling with the implications of his words. "Lorien," she whispered, hardly daring to believe what she was hearing.

"I know it's wrong," he continued, his voice rough with emotion. "I know that everything about this goes against what I've been taught, what I've always believed. But I can't help it. When I'm with you, I feel... alive in a way I never have before. Like I'm seeing the world through new eyes."

Elara's heart ached at the vulnerability in his tone, the raw honesty of his confession. She wished more than anything that she could turn and face him, look into his eyes and tell him that she understood, that she was feeling the same way. But the binding spell held her fast, trapping her in place.

"I'm scared, Elara," Lorien whispered. "I don't know what this means, or where it could lead. I've never felt like this before, and I don't know how to navigate it."

Elara swallowed hard, blinking back the sudden sting of tears. "I'm scared too," she confessed, her voice trembling.

"I've been trying to ignore it, to convince myself that what I'm feeling isn't real. But the truth is, I can't stop thinking about you. About the way you see the world, the way you make me question everything I thought I knew."

As if sensing her need, the binding spell suddenly relaxed its hold, allowing Elara to shift and turn in Lorien's arms until they were face to face. She gazed up at him, her heart racing as she took in the ethereal beauty of his features, the way his luminescent markings glowed in the dim light of the room.

"And I," she breathed, reaching up to cup his cheek with a trembling hand. "This connection between us, this pull that I can't explain. But I'm afraid. Afraid that it's not real, that it's just the spell playing tricks on our minds and hearts."

Lorien leaned into her touch, his eyes fluttering closed for a moment as he savored the sensation of her skin against his. "I know," he murmured, his voice rough with emotion. "I've been wondering the same thing. But Elara..."

His voice trailed off as he stroked her face.

Elara's breath hitched in her throat, her heart swelling with a fierce, desperate hope. "How can you be sure?" she whispered, searching his face for any hint of doubt or hesitation.

Lorien's gaze held hers, unwavering and intense. "I don't know," he whispered. "I just know what I feel right now."

And as they gazed into each other's eyes, the rest of the world didn't exist, leaving only the two of them, lost in a moment of perfect understanding and connection.

Lorien leaned in, closing the distance between them until his lips hovered a mere breath away from Elara's. Her heart raced, anticipation coursing through her veins as she felt the warmth of his skin, the soft caress of his breath against her face. And then, with a gentleness that belied the intensity of his desire, Lorien pressed his lips to hers in a tender, passionate kiss.

Elara melted into his embrace, her body molding itself to his as she lost herself in the sensation of his mouth moving against hers. His lips were soft, yet insistent, and she parted her own in a silent invitation, letting him deepen the kiss until she was breathless and dizzy with longing.

As they kissed, Lorien's hands began to roam over her body, tracing the curves of her waist and hips with a reverence that made her shiver. Elara's own hands were busy exploring the planes of his back, marveling at the strength she could feel in his muscles, the smoothness of his skin beneath her fingertips. Her hands caressed his wings, which were neatly folded in, laying outside of his shirt. At first she pulled her hands away, but he didn't seem bothered.

Slowly, almost hesitantly, they began to undress each other, their movements gentle and unhurried as they savored each new revelation of skin. Elara's breath caught in her throat as Lorien's shirt fell away, revealing the intricate patterns of his luminescent markings, which seemed to pulse and glow in response to her touch.

"You're beautiful," she whispered, tracing the lines with trembling fingers. "Like nothing I've ever seen before."

Lorien smiled, a tender, almost shy expression that made her heart ache with a fierce protectiveness. "As are you," he murmured, his gaze roaming over her body with undisguised admiration. "I never thought a human could be so exquisite."

As they continued to explore each other's bodies, Elara couldn't help but discern the subtle differences between Lorien and the human men she had known. His skin was cooler to the touch, almost like silk, and there was a faint, shimmering aura that appeared to emanate from his very pores. She could sense the magic thrumming through his veins, a palpable energy that set her own blood on fire.

He knelt on the bed and stretched his wings out. With the moonlight streaming in they were beautiful.

"Can I- Can I touch them?" Elara asked hesitantly.

Lorien smiled, eyes full of desire. "You can touch any part of me you'd like."

He took one of her hands and showed her how to stroke the outlining structure of them. "I like this," was all he added.

Elara saw his eyes roll back in desire, and melodious hum, turned deep a feral was how he demanded for her to continue stroking. Elara felt her womanly parts pulse in response to his sound.

Elara leaned in close, her breath mingling with Lorien's as their bodies pressed together. The heat of his arousal against her thigh sent a shiver of anticipation down her spine. His hands roamed over her back, tracing patterns of fire on her skin.

As their passion grew, Elara found herself lost in a haze of sensation. Lorien's touch was electric, igniting every nerve ending until she felt like she might combust from the sheer intensity of it all. She arched into him, desperate for more contact, more friction, more of everything he had to offer.

But just as they were on the brink of taking that final step, Elara forced herself to pull back. Her heart was racing, her body screaming at her to continue, but she knew they couldn't rush this. Not when there was so much at stake.

"Wait," she gasped, her voice hoarse with desire. "We can't... not yet."

Lorien's eyes were dark with hunger, but he nodded in understanding. "You're right," he said tenderly, brushing a strand of hair from her face. "We need to be sure of what we're feeling. I don't want to risk hurting you."

Elara's heart swelled with emotion. She realized it couldn't have been easy for him to stop, not when they were both so caught up in the moment. But the fact that he was willing to put her needs first spoke volumes about his character.

They held each other close, their bodies still thrumming with unspent desire. But there was a new sense of intimacy between them now, a deeper understanding of what they meant to each other.

"We'll take this slow," Lorien promised, his voice a soothing balm to her soul. "We have all the time in the world to explore what we have together."

Elara nodded, burying her face in the crook of his neck. She knew their journey was just beginning, but with Lorien by her side, she felt like she could face anything. As long as they had each other, nothing else mattered.

Chapter 11

A PARADE OF COLOR DANCED through the enchanted forest as the Festival of Light burst to life. Fairies of every hue flitted between the glowing lanterns strung from tree to tree, their laughter mingling with festive music. There were more fairies than Elara could have imagined. Lorien told her that some were visitors from other areas, just here for the festival.

Amidst the joyous revelry, Elara Mariposa Santiago emerged like a vision from a dream. Her gown, a masterpiece of shimmering gossamer and delicate lace, floated around her as if carried by an unseen breeze. The bodice clung to her curves, celebrating her womanly figure, while the skirt cascaded in gentle waves, brushing against her smooth, sun-kissed skin with each graceful step.

Elara's rich, ebony curls were piled atop her head in an elegant updo adorned with twinkling gemstones that caught the light like stars plucked from the night sky. A few artful tendrils escaped to frame her face, softening the striking planes of her features. She had rich, curly dark hair that cascaded over her shoulders and warm, mahogany-toned skin, and her smile was a melody of cultural richness, echoing a heritage of diverse, vibrant ancestors. Her hazel eyes, flecked with gold, shone with wonder as she drank in the enchanting sights and sounds that surrounded her.

As she navigated the bustling crowd, Elara couldn't contain her amazement. She turned to Lorien, who walked closely beside her, and exclaimed, "Can you believe the royal seamstress created this dress so quickly? It's like she plucked the vision straight from my dreams and wove it into reality!"

She twirled, and the dress's colors spun like a kaleidoscope.

Lorien smiled, his eyes warm with affection as he gazed upon Elara. "With magic, nearly anything is possible in our realm. And you, Elara, are a vision of loveliness that outshines even the most radiant faerie here tonight."

A blush bloomed across Elara's cheeks at the compliment. She ducked her head shyly before meeting Lorien's gaze once more. "Thank you. It is as if I'm walking through a dream, surrounded by such beauty and wonder."

As they continued through the festival, Elara couldn't help but marvel at the intricate details of her gown. The bodice was embroidered with shimmering thread that depicted swirling vines and delicate blossoms that were actually alive. Lorien said they'd grow, bloom, or shimmer whenever she performed in it. The skirt was adorned with countless tiny crystals that caught the light with every movement. It was a dress fit for a princess, yet it embraced Elara's unique style and celebrated her heritage in a way that made her feel really seen and cherished.

Elara's heart swelled with gratitude and excitement as she looked ahead to their upcoming performance. With Lorien by her side and the magic of the Festival of Light all around them, she appreciated that this night would be one she would never forget.

From a distance, Aria observed the pair with a critical eye, her features marred by a frown. The way Lorien gazed at Elara, the gentle touches and secret smiles they shared, sent a bitter pang through her heart. She had always believed that Lorien would one day see her as more than just a friend and advisor, but now it appeared that his affections were fixed on the human woman.

ARIA'S FINGERS CLENCHED around the delicate fabric of her gown as she fought to keep her emotions in check. Through her tireless research, she had discovered the key to breaking the binding spell that tethered Lorien to Elara. It would be so simple to approach them now, to reveal what she knew and watch as the spell unraveled, freeing Lorien from his obligation.

But something held her back. A small, insistent voice whispered that to do so would be to betray Lorien's trust, to undermine his authority as the prince of the Fae. And yet, the jealousy that coiled in her gut refused to be silenced. Aria closed her eyes, drawing in a deep breath as she wrestled with the warring impulses within her.

When she opened her eyes again, Lorien and Elara had disappeared into the crowd, their laughter echoing faintly on the breeze. Aria's jaw tightened with resolve. She would bide her time, watch, and wait for the perfect moment to act. For now, she would play the role of the loyal friend and advisor, but when the time was right, she would do whatever it took to claim Lorien's heart for her own.

At the same time, Thorne wove through the festival-goers, his dark hair and violet eyes a stark contrast to the vibrant hues of the gathered Fae. His lips curled into a smirk as he leaned close to a group of young fairies, his voice low and conspiratorial.

"Have you seen the way our prince fawns over the human girl?" he murmured, his eyebrows raised in mock concern. "It's hardly befitting of a future ruler, don't you think?"

The fairies exchanged glances, their expressions a mix of surprise and unease. One of them, a petite blonde with delicate features, frowned as she observed Lorien and Elara from across the clearing.

"It does seem rather inappropriate," she agreed, her voice tinged with disapproval. "What could he possibly see in her?"

Thorne's smirk widened as he sensed the seeds of doubt taking root. He moved on to another group, his words carefully chosen to fan the flames of discontent.

As he continued his subtle campaign, he caught sight of Taliesin approaching Lorien and Elara, his blue hair shimmering in the sunlight. Thorne's eyes narrowed, recognizing the potential threat to his plans. Lorien has as many loyal friends as Thorne had followers.

Taliesin, however, was oblivious to the growing tension in the air. He greeted the couple with a broad grin, his eyes sparkling with mirth.

"Well, if it isn't the talk of the festival!" he exclaimed, clapping Lorien on the shoulder. "I must say, you two make quite the striking pair."

Elara blushed, ducking her head as she smiled shyly. "Thank you, Taliesin. I'm so out of place here, but Lorien has been wonderful."

Lorien's gaze softened as he looked at her, his hand instinctively seeking hers. "You belong here, Elara. You literally belong wherever I am."

Taliesin's grin widened as he regarded the exchange. "I've never seen you quite so smitten, my friend," he teased, his tone good-natured. "It suits you."

Lorien laughed, the sound warm and rich. "I suppose it does," he agreed, his eyes never leaving Elara's face.

Thorne, watching from the shadows, was irritated at the easy camaraderie between the three. He scowled, his mind racing as he sought a new angle of attack.

But Taliesin, as if sensing the growing unease, chose that moment to step forward, his voice ringing out clear and strong.

"Friends, let us not forget the true purpose of this festival," he called, his arms and wings spread wide. "We gather to celebrate the light, to revel in the magic that binds us all. Let our differences fall away, and let us come together in joy and unity."

A cheer rose from the crowd, the tension broken by Taliesin's words. Elara smiled and leaned into Lorien's side as the fairies began to dance and sing again.

Thorne slipped into the shadows, his fake smile barely concealing his rage. He realized any other undermining talk right after that would make him look bad instead of the prince. But he would not be so easily deterred. He vowed to himself that one way or another, he would see Lorien's downfall, and Elara would be the key.

As the festival peaked, Elara and Lorien found themselves drawn to a secluded corner of the grounds, away from the prying eyes of the crowd. The music muted here, the laughter distant as if they had stepped into a world of their own making.

Elara leaned against a tree, her gown shimmering in the dappled light. "I can't believe this is happening," she murmured, her eyes wide with wonder. "It's like something out of a dream."

Lorien smiled, his gaze soft as he looked at her. "And yet, it's real," he said, reaching out to tuck a stray curl behind her ear. His fingers lingered on her cheek, sending a shiver down her spine. "You're real."

Elara's heart skipped a beat at his touch and the intensity of his gaze. She had never experienced these emotions before, this sense of connection, of belonging. It was as if she had been waiting her whole life for this moment, for him.

Since their binding they had talked for hours, sharing their hopes and dreams, their fears and doubts. Elara spoke of her love for music and her desire to bring joy to others through her playing. Lorien listened diligently, his eyes never leaving her face, as if he were committing every detail to memory.

In turn, he shared his dreams and his vision for a future where fairies and humans could live in harmony with the natural world he loved, and the barriers between their worlds would crumble away. Elara felt herself drawn into his words, into the passion and conviction that burned in his eyes.

As they talked, stolen glances passed between them, each one filled with a longing that neither could quite put into words. Elara heart raced, and skin tingled with every brush of Lorien's hand against hers.

Around them, the festival continued, the music swelling to a crescendo as the anticipation for their performance grew. Whispers spread through the crowd, tales of the Fae Prince and the human woman who would sing together, their voices intertwined in a duet that would be remembered for generations.

Elara felt a flicker of nerves at the thought of performing before so many, but one look at Lorien's face, at the trust and belief that shone in his eyes, and she felt her fears melt away. With him by her side, she knew she could face anything.

As their performance drew near, Lorien took Elara's hand, his fingers lacing with hers. "Are you ready?" he asked.

Elara nodded, a smile spreading across her face. "Getting there."Sensing her anxiety, Lorien led Elara further away from the bustling crowd, guiding her through a maze of enchanted trees and glowing flowers until they reached a secluded alcove. The soft strains of music from the festival drifted through the air, mingling with the gentle rustling of leaves overhead.

Elara's heart raced as Lorien turned to face her, his eyes filled with a tenderness that took her breath away. "Elara," he murmured, leaning in close so she could feel his warm breath, "I want you to know that no matter what happens out there, I believe in you. Your music, your voice... they have a magic all their own."

A smile tugged at Elara's lips, her nerves beginning to settle in the face of Lorien's unwavering support. "Thank you," she whispered, her fingers intertwining with his. "I never could have imagined any of this... performing for the Fae Royalty, being here with you..."

Lorien's free hand came up to cup her cheek, his thumb lightly tracing the curve of her jawline. "And to think, you'll be performing with one of them, too," he teased, a playful grin spreading across his face.

Elara laughed, leaning into his touch.

Slowly, as if drawn by an invisible force, they leaned in, their lips meeting in a passionate kiss. Elara's heart raced, and her body molded to Lorien's as his arms encircled her waist, pulling her closer. The kiss deepened, their tongues dancing, exploring, as the heat between them grew.

Unbeknownst to the entwined lovers, a pair of violet eyes kept an eye from the shadows. Thorne's lips curled into a smirk, his gaze calculating as he observed the intimate moment. This, he knew, was a weakness he could exploit, a chink in the armor of the future Fae King.

Just as Thorne prepared to confront Lorien and Elara, a commotion erupted at the edge of the festival grounds. Two Fae guards, their armor glinting in the soft glow of the faerie lights, marched into the crowd, their hands firmly grasping the arms of two struggling humans. Alerted by the commotion, the two lovers came back among the crowd to see the cause.

Elara's eyes widened, her heart leaping into her throat as she recognized the familiar faces. "Dante? Cassie?" she whispered, her voice laced with disbelief and worry.

Immediately, she tried to run to her brother, to wrap him in a fierce hug and demand an explanation for his sudden appearance. But the moment she stepped forward, the binding spell tightened, anchoring her to Lorien's side.

Lorien, his posture stiffening, refused to move. His eyes, once filled with warmth and affection, now hardened with suspicion and anger. The same hatred that marred his features during their first encounter returned.

Elara's heart sank as she realized the spell was drawing them even closer together, their bodies nearly touching. She could sense tension radiating from Lorien, his muscles coiled like a spring ready to snap.

"Let me go to them. They're my family!"

But Lorien remained unmoved, his gaze fixed on the approaching guards and their human captives. "They shouldn't be here. This is a Fae celebration, not a place for humans to intrude."

Elara's eyes filled with tears, her excitement at seeing her loved ones tempered by the growing unease in her chest. She glanced around, searching for a friendly face, someone who could intervene and defuse the situation.

Her gaze landed on Queen Isadora, who stood at the edge of the crowd, her expression a mix of concern and curiosity. Internally, Elara implored the queen for help, hoping her kind nature would prevail over the rising tide of tension.

As the guards dragged Dante and Cassie into the center of the festival grounds, the music faltered, the laughter died away, and an eerie silence descended upon the gathered Fae. All eyes turned to the humans, their presence a stark reminder of the fragile peace between their realms.

Elara's heart raced, her mind whirling with questions and fears. What had brought Dante and Cassie to the Fae kingdom? Why had they been restrained? And most importantly, how could she bridge the growing divide between the man she loved and the family she cherished?

The air crackled with tension, the weight of the unfolding events pressing on Elara's shoulders. She grasped that the next few moments would be crucial, that the fate of her relationships, and perhaps even the future of the Fae and human realms, hung in the balance.

Cassie, her eyes wide with a mix of fear and determination, spoke first. "We got lost in the forest. We were searching for Elara, and we stumbled upon the faerie castle. We didn't mean any harm."

Dante nodded, his gaze locked on Elara. "We were worried about you, sis. When we received Lord Lorien's message, it wasn't well received back home. Dad... he's not happy."

Elara's heart sank at the mention of her father's displeasure. She knew his distrust of the Fae ran deep, but she had hoped that Lorien's message would have reassured him of her safety and happiness.

Lorien, sensing Elara's distress, stepped forward. The binding spell tugged at him, urging him to remain close to her, but he fought against it, his need to protect her overriding the magic's pull. He addressed the guards, his voice steady and commanding. "Release them. They are guests in our realm and shall be treated as such."

The guards hesitated momentarily, their eyes darting between Lorien and the humans. But as they caught sight of the queen's approving nod, they relented, releasing their grip on Dante and Cassie.

The spell's restraint loosened, allowing Elara to rush forward and throw her arms around Dante in a fierce hug. Tears pricked at the corners of her eyes as she held him close, the relief of his presence washing over her. Cassie joined the embrace, her tears mingling with Elara's.

"I'm so glad you're here," Elara whispered, her voice thick with emotion. "I've missed you both so much."

As she pulled back, Elara's eyes sparkled with excitement. "You won't believe how beautiful this kingdom is and how kind the Fae have been to me. It's like a dream come true."

She gestured towards the queen, who observed the reunion with a warm smile. "Queen Everoak has been so welcoming, and the Fae have embraced me as one of their own."

Dante and Cassie exchanged a glance, their expressions a mix of relief and uncertainty. They understood that Hector's fears would not be easily assuaged, but seeing Elara's happiness and the queen's kindness gave them hope that perhaps a bridge could be built between their worlds.

Lorien approached the group, his eyes softening as he took in the scene. The binding spell, sensing the easing of tensions, loosened its grip, allowing him to stand a comfortable distance from Elara. He placed a gentle hand on her shoulder, a silent show of support and affection.

Elara leaned into his touch, drawing strength from his presence.

Cassie's voice cut through the joyful reunion, her tone grave and urgent. "Elara, I'm sorry, but we must tell you something."

The mood shifted abruptly as all eyes turned to Cassie. Elara's smile faltered, a sense of dread creeping into her heart.

"What is it?" she asked.

Dante stepped forward, his brow furrowed with concern. "A mob of angry villagers is on their way here, led by Father. They think the Fae have kidnapped you, and they're coming to rescue you."

Elara's eyes widened in shock, her hand automatically reaching for Lorien's. The binding spell tightened, drawing them closer as if sensing the impending danger.

"But that's not true!" Elara exclaimed, her voice trembling. "I'm here of my own free will. The Fae have been nothing but kind to me."

Dante shook his head. "We got lost, so we're only just a bit ahead of them. They could be here anytime."

Lorien's grip tightened and his jaw clenched. "We won't let them take you, Elara. We'll find a way to protect you and maintain the peace between our realms."

Both that there were spellbound and spoke as if they had a choice.

The festival-goers began to murmur amongst themselves, their joyous laughter replaced by worried whispers and uneasy glances toward the forest. The queen's smile faded.

Elara's mind raced with possibilities, her heart torn between her love for her family and her newfound connection to the Fae. She knew that the fragile harmony between their worlds hung in the balance, and one wrong move could shatter it forever.

Chapter 12

AS IF ON CUE, THE TRANQUIL enchantment of the Festival of Light shattered as Hector and a group of disheveled villagers burst through the treeline, their faces etched with urgency and determination. Elara's heart leapt into her throat at the sight of her father, his usually neat hair wild and his eyes darting frantically across the gathering.

"Elara!" Hector's voice boomed across the clearing, raw with desperation. "Elara, where are you?"

Elara pressed closer to Lorien, her hands grasping his arm. She could feel the tension radiating off him as he turned to face the approaching villagers, his body a protective shield between her and the chaos.

Around them, startled gasps and murmurs rippled through the crowd of fairies and humans alike. They had only just heard Dante's warning when they were immediately faced with it's reality. Elara's heart raced as she saw her father shouldering his way through the stunned revelers, his gaze locked on Lorien.

"Father, wait!" Elara called out, her voice trembling. "What are you doing?"

But Hector seemed not to hear her, his face contorted with a mix of anger and fear as he finally reached them. Up close, Elara could see the scratches on his arms and the leaves tangled in his hair, as if he had fought his way through the forest itself to get here.

"Get away from my daughter," Hector growled, reaching out to grab Elara's arm.

Lorien's hand shot out, catching Hector's wrist in an iron grip. "Elara is here of her own free will. There's no need for this aggression." Hector wrenched his arm free, his eyes flashing. He tried to swing at Lorien who ducked. "I know better than to trust your kind. I'm taking her home where she belongs, away from your enchantments and trickery."

Elara's mind raced as she tried to make sense of her father's sudden appearance and hostile demeanor.

She stepped forward, placing herself between the two bristling men. "Father, please. Lorien means me no harm. If you would just listen -"

"No, Elara." Hector's voice was hard and unyielding. "I've seen the evil these creatures are capable of. I won't let you fall victim to their wiles like your mother..."

He trailed off, his face twisting with a grief and rage that made Elara's breath catch. In all her years, she had never seen such raw, anguished emotion from her stoic father.

Hector's gaze shifted back to Lorien, his eyes narrowing. "Let her go! Or I swear by all that is holy, you'll regret the day you laid eyes on my daughter."

Around them, the crowd held its collective breath, the tension crackling like electricity in the air. Elara's heart ached as she stood torn between the two worlds, the man she loved and the father she would do almost anything to see happy. She knew she had to find a way to bridge this divide before it tore them all apart.

As if sensing Elara's inner turmoil, the spell between her and Lorien suddenly intensified, pulling them closer until they stood shoulder to shoulder, their hands intertwined. A soft gasp escaped Elara's lips as she felt Lorien's skin against hers, the thrum of his heartbeat echoing her own.

Hector's eyes widened in disbelief and fury. "What is this sorcery?" he bellowed, lunging forward to wrench them apart. His hands grasped at their arms, but the spell held fast, unyielding.

Elara couldn't help but let out a breathless laugh at the almost comical sight of her father struggling against the enchantment. "Father, stop! You're only making it worse."

But Hector wasn't listening. He grunted with effort, his face turning red as he strained to separate them. Lorien's grip on her hands tighten in a subtle warning.

"Enough." Lorien's voice was low, edged with a quiet anger that sent a shiver down Elara's spine. "I will not allow you to be so rough with Elara again. She is not a child to be manhandled at your whim."

Hector staggered back as if struck, his chest heaving. For a moment, Elara thought he might back down and reason. But then his face hardened, a vein pulsing in his temple.

"You dare presume to tell me how to treat my own daughter?" He spun to face the other villagers, his arm sweeping out in a grand gesture. "Are we to stand idly by while these creatures bewitch our children, our loved ones? I say we take back what is ours!"

A chorus of shouts erupted from the crowd as the villagers surged forward, brandishing makeshift weapons. Elara's heart sank. She knew they stood no chance against the powerful magic of the fairies, but she couldn't bear the thought of anyone getting hurt, especially not because of her.

The fairies moved with a fluid grace, the very air around them shimmering with power. Vines burst from the ground, entangling the villagers' feet. Gusts of wind sent some of them tumbling backwards. The forest itself seemed to come alive, the trees groaning and creaking as they bent to the fairies' will. Some of the humans and fairies were engaged in scuffles, of which the humans were on the losing side. They had to know they had no chance against a fae in a physical brawl, yet they fought.

And through it all, Elara stood frozen, Lorien's presence at her side the only thing keeping her grounded. She watched helplessly as her father and the other villagers were beaten back, their efforts futile against the might of the forest.

Oh, father, if only you could see that not all fairies are to be feared. If only you could understand the love I have for Lorien, for this magical world.

Just as the chaos reached a fevered pitch, a commanding voice rang out across the clearing. "Stop!"

The Queen walked forward, her presence radiating an aura of calm authority. The fighting ceased immediately, humans and fairies alike turning to face the regal figure.

"On this day, the Festival of Light, a time of unity and celebration, you dare bring violence to our realm?" The Queen's words were not harsh, but firm, her gaze sweeping over the assembled crowd.

Elara marveled at the Queen's composure, the way she seemed to command respect without raising her voice.

The Queen's eyes settled on Cassie and Dante, standing apart from the other villagers. "I see not all of you arrived with hatred in your hearts. The forest recognized this, allowing you passage unscathed."

Elara glanced at her brother and friend, noting the absence of scratches and bruises that marred the other villagers. A flicker of hope ignited within her. Perhaps there was still a chance for understanding between their two worlds.

The Queen then turned her attention to the rest of the villagers, her expression softening. "I sense great pain and loss driving your actions. But I implore you, do not let grief cloud your judgment. The Festival of Light is a time for letting go of the past and embracing a brighter future."

Hector stepped forward, his face reflecting years of hurt. "How dare you speak of our pain as if you understand it?" His voice trembled, years of bottled-up emotions spilling forth. "Your kind took my wife, my Elara's mother. She ventured into your forest, and she never returned. You speak of letting go, but how can I, when the memory of her loss haunts me every day?"

Hector's voice broke as he spoke, his eyes brimming with unshed tears. A pang of sadness hit Elara's heart and she reached for his hand, knowing the pain and grief that had consumed him all this time.

"I can't believe it's been sixteen years since that day. The day my Elara arrived home alone, without her mother."

"She told me she heard something beautiful from your forest. Your forest lured her in, and her mother, my love, Mariposa followed her to get her back," Hector continued, his voice wavering. "Because lord knows we aren't allowed pass the line into *your* side of the forest. But before Elara could find the sound, she found an Orc scout...and everything changed. My wife used her music to distract the creature and told Elara to run, sacrificing herself to save our child." His voice was a whisper now, choked with anguish.

Elara squeezed her father's hand tighter, offering comfort as she listened to the pain in his words. "We searched for days, but she never emerged from the forest. We even begged the Fae for help, but you refused and denied us access into *your* part of the forest."

Anger flashed in Hector's eyes as he thought of the Fairies' betrayal. "You not only turned their backs on us when we needed you most, but you allowed such a dangerous creature to roam freely in your territory!" he exclaimed, his voice rising with each word. Tears finally spilled down his cheeks as he finished telling his tragic story.

Elara's heart clenched at her father's words, a wave of guilt washing over her. *He still blames himself and he blames the Fae.*

She tried to push back the thought, but couldn't. *He probably blames me too.*

She wanted to reach out to him, to offer comfort, but the words stuck in her throat.

For the first time in sixteen years Elara thought of the sound she'd heard that lured her into the forest as a child. She couldn't help but compare how a sound had lured her into the forest again.

Was it a Fae she'd heard as a child? Was is Lorien? Was it the forest itself?

But she couldn't ponder this thoughts, putting them off for later as she cast her eyes on the tense faces of the humans who had accompanied Hector. She knew what the Fae were now hearing—they has a reason for the fear and hatred they felt, even if it was misplaced.

The Queen's expression softened further, compassion etched into her ageless features. "I am truly sorry for your loss. The grief of losing a loved one is a heavy burden to bear. But tell me, what gives you the right to make such horrible assumptions about the Fae? Have we not always strived for peace between our realms?"

Hector's eyes flashed with defiance. "Peace?" He scoffed. "My wife sought peace, and look what it brought her. Death at the hands of and Orc and no sympathy from your kind."

He turned to Elara, his gaze a mixture of accusation and desperation. "Have you learned nothing my daughter? The Fae cannot be trusted. They lure us in with their magic and beauty, only to destroy us in the end."

Elara's heart raced as all eyes turned to her, the weight of her father's words settling heavily on her shoulders. She was torn, caught between her love for her father and her growing understanding of the Fae.

How can I make him see? How can I show him that there is goodness in this world, too?

The Queen followed the exchange without a word, her ancient eyes seeming to peer into the very depths of their souls. Elara sensed that she understood the situation's complexity and the deep-rooted pain and mistrust that divided their people. *But how do we move forward?* Elara thought. *How do we heal these wounds and find a way to coexist in peace?*

Lorien's brow furrowed as he turned to Elara, his luminescent eyes filled with hurt and confusion. "Elara, you never told me about your mother. I thought we had grown close, that we shared a bond of trust."

Elara's heart ached at the pain in his voice. She reached out to him, her fingers trembling as they brushed against his arm. "Lorien, I'm so sorry. I didn't know how to bring it up. The pain of losing her... it's still so raw. And there is so much of it I have forgotten. I was a child. The forest sounds luring me in. The face of the monster that killed my mother as it emerged from the trees. I tried to forget."

She took a deep breath, gathering her courage. "But my father is right. While the Fae have certainly been given good reason to mistrust humans, some humans have a good reason not to trust the Fae. My mother's death... it changed everything for us."

Lorien's gaze softened, and he gently took Elara's hand. "I understand," he murmured, "but we cannot let the past define our future. We must find a way to move forward, to build bridges instead of walls."

Elara nodded, a glimmer of hope sparking in her chest.

She turned to her father, her eyes shining with hope. "Father, I know you're hurting. I know you want to protect me. But we cannot let fear and hatred guide us. We must be willing to open our hearts, to see the good in others, even when it's difficult. We have no idea why the Fae wouldn't let us in. My time here has privy me to the fact that Orc are no friends of the Fairies, and there is no way that Orc had permission to be there. The faeries probably didn't know about the Orc until then, and they've been fighting them. Maybe my mother, as important as she was to us, was just a blip in the bigger picture they couldn't deal with. One woman, as loved as she was, or a whole kingdom?"

Hector's stern expression faltered, and for a moment, Elara saw a flicker of the man he had once been - the loving father who had taught her to see the beauty in the world. *There is still hope for him*, she realized, *still a chance for us to find our way back to each other.*

A knowing smile played at the corners of the Queen's lips.

With a graceful wave of her hand, the Queen's enchantment swept over the gathered humans, compelling them to sit where they stood. Hector sank to the ground, his limbs heavy and unwilling to obey his commands. Around him, the other villagers, their faces etched with a mix of fear and confusion, succumbed to the same fate.

Elara alone remained standing, her hazel eyes wide with wonder and apprehension.

The Queen's voice, melodic and commanding, filled the air. "It is time for the performance," she announced, her gaze settling on Elara and Lorien. "Let us see what fate have in store for us."

A hush fell over the gathered crowd. The two walked to the circular area where performers were staged. Elara's fingers twitched, longing to pluck the strings of her instrument and pour her heart into the music. *This is our chance to show them the power of unity, the beauty that can arise when two worlds collide.*

Beside her, Lorien stood tall, his presence a reassuring anchor amid the chaos. Their eyes met, and a silent conversation passed between them. His gaze seemed to say "Together, we can face whatever comes next."

As the Queen stepped back, gesturing for them to take center stage, Elara drew a deep breath. The weight of the moment settled on her shoulders, but so too did the exhilaration of the challenge ahead.

This is our story, she thought, *and we will write it in harmony.*

Elara and Lorien moved in perfect sync as the spell that bound them loosened just enough to allow their performance. Elara's fingers danced across the strings of her instrument, the first notes ringing out clear and true. Lorien's voice soon joined her, his rich baritone weaving through the melody like a river through a forest.

Their duet was ethereal, a harmonious blend of human and fae magic that seemed to fill the very air around them. Elara's heartfelt lyrics spoke of a love transcending boundaries, of two hearts finding each other against all odds.

"In the shadows of the forest deep,
Where ancient secrets lie in sleep,
Two souls entwined, a bond so rare,
A love that blooms, beyond compare."

As the music swelled, Elara began to move, her body flowing with the rhythm of their song. Her interpretive dance was visual poetry, each gesture and step telling the story of their journey together. She spun and leapt, her skirts swirling around her like a kaleidoscope of color, her movements expressing the joy and wonder of their connection. The magic woven through the dress made it come alive, the vines shimmering as small flowers began to open, revealing tiny hidden jewels.

"Through the murky depths of ancient woods,
Where secrets whispered through the broods,
Two hearts entwined, amidst the night,
A love that glows, forever bright.
In starlit glades and moonlit paths,
Their love a flame that never wanes,
A bond so true, it cannot be tamed,
For in each other's arms they're claimed.
Amidst the shadows, their passion blooms,
Like wildflowers in a hidden tomb,
Their souls dance to a timeless tune,
Beneath the stars and pale blue moon."

The crowd watched, transfixed, as the duo's performance unfolded. The humans and fairies alike were drawn into the moment's magic, their hearts stirring with the power of the music. Yet, even as many were swept away by the scene's beauty, others watched with mixed emotions.

Dante and Taliesin exchanged excited grins, their eyes alight with pride and mischief as they witnessed the impact of Elara and Lorien's duet. But Hector's face remained stony, his eyes narrowed in suspicion and disapproval. Thorne's expression was one of poorly concealed contempt, his lips twisted into a sneer as he observed the display of unity.

And Aria, the faerie whose heart had once belonged to Lorien, watched with longing and heartbreak. Her ice-blue eyes glistened with unshed tears as she witnessed the undeniable bond between the human girl and the fae prince, a love she had once hoped to call her own.

As the final notes of their song faded into the air, Elara and Lorien stood hand in hand, their chests heaving with exertion and emotion. The spell that had loosened for their performance started threading tightly around them again. The ensuing silence was pregnant with anticipation, the crowd seeming to hold its breath as they awaited the response to this unprecedented display of unity.

And then, like a dam bursting, the applause erupted. Humans and fairies alike rose to their feet, their cheers and claps thundering through the air. It was a moment of triumph, a testament to the power of love and the possibility of peace between their two worlds.

But even as the applause washed over them, Elara couldn't shake the feeling that their greatest challenges still lay ahead. She squeezed Lorien's hand.

For now, though, we will revel in this victory, and face whatever comes next together.

As the applause began to die, a hush fell over the crowd as Queen Everoak gracefully walked toward the pair, her gown trailing behind her. Elara and Lorien turned to face her, their hands still intertwined, a mixture of trepidation and hope flickering in their eyes.

The Queen's gaze swept over the young couple, a gentle smile playing at the corners of her lips. "My dear children, your performance tonight has touched the hearts of all who witnessed it. The love and unity you have shown in the face of such adversity is a testament to the power of the bond you share."

She placed a hand on each of their shoulders, her touch radiating warmth and acceptance. "Elara, your bravery and compassion have shown us that the human spirit is capable of great things. And Lorien, your willingness to open your heart to one from beyond our realm is a shining example of the capacity for growth and understanding within us all."

Tears prickled at the corners of Elara's eyes, overwhelmed by the Queen's words and the significance of this moment. *She called us her children,* she thought, her heart swelling with emotion. *She sees us as equals, as part of her family.*

The Queen drew them both into a warm embrace, her arms encircling them with a mother's love. At that moment, Elara felt a sense of belonging, a connection to something greater than herself.

But even as they basked in the glow of the Queen's approval, a sudden, chilling sensation washed over Elara, Lorien, and the Queen. It was as if the air around them had shifted, a subtle but unmistakable change that sent shivers down their spines.

The spell, Elara realized, her eyes widening in shock. *It's breaking.*

She looked to Lorien and the Queen, seeing the same realization dawning on their faces. The rest of the crowd seemed oblivious, still caught up in the moment's excitement; but for the three of them, the world had suddenly tilted on its axis.

What does this mean? Elara wondered, fear and uncertainty coiling in her gut. *And what will happen now that the spell is unraveling?*

Chapter 13

AS THE FESTIVAL CAME to a close, fairies and humans alike began to disperse, their laughter and chatter fading into the warm evening air. Elara and Lorien stood together at the edge of the festivities, their hands brushing gingerly against each other. Though the binding spell had been broken, an invisible force still seemed to draw them together.

A group of fairies led by Oakley fluttered over to the couple, their wings glittering in the fading sunlight. "Prince Lorien, Lady Elara, that was an enchanting performance," he said with a bow. "Your connection was palpable. I hope you perform at the next festival!"

"Yes, even for a human," said a small fae boy who looked very much like his father.

Oakley gave him a slap in the back of the head. "Mind ya manners."

The boy, who Elara could only guess was very young, though it was hard to tell with fairies, gave an impish grin.

"I was just playing!" He flew closer to Elara and opened his palm, and like magic, a small flower full of colors bloomed. He gave it to Elara with a grin. "Matches your dress!" he said before returning to his father's side.

Elara curtsied, a huge grin on her face. "Why, thank you!"

"Yes, it was amazing!" Dante who stood nearby said. "I knew you were good—but mom would have been proud! You too," he added, looking at Lorien.

Elara blushed, glancing shyly at Lorien. His green eyes sparkled with affection as he returned her gaze. "Thank you."

As the group of fairies took their leave, Elara's attention was drawn to a group of human villagers clustered nearby. They shifted uncomfortably, eyeing the surrounding fairies with curiosity and apprehension. Some fairies approached them tentatively, offering friendly smiles and gestures of goodwill.

An elderly faerie with kind eyes extended a hand to a wary-looking farmer. "We mean you no harm. Perhaps we could share stories of our lands and traditions," she said.

The farmer hesitated for a momentarily before accepting her hand. His weathered face softened. Other villagers followed suit, conversing cautiously with the fairies who had approached them.

Elara's heart swelled with hope at the sight. It was a small step, but it promised a more harmonious future. She turned to Lorien, her eyes shining. "Do you think this is the beginning of something new?" she asked softly. "A chance for our peoples to indeed understand each other?"

Lorien squeezed her hand reassuringly. "I believe it is. Change takes time, but today, we have shown that it is possible. Your bravery and compassion have inspired us all."

Despite the warmth of his words, Elara couldn't shake the lingering unease in her heart. She knew that her father and the other villagers would soon expect her to return home, to leave behind this magical realm and the love she had found within it. The thought filled her with a bittersweet ache.

As if sensing her inner turmoil, Lorien pulled her close, his arms encircling her waist. "We'll find a way," he whispered, his breath tickling her ear.

Elara leaned into his embrace.

Suddenly, a familiar voice cut through the air, shattering the delicate peace of the moment. "Elara! It's time to go home. Now."

Elara tensed, her heart sinking as she turned to face her father. His brow was furrowed, and his stance rigid. "Papa, please," she pleaded, her voice trembling. "Can't we talk about this? I... I'm not ready to leave yet."

Hector's gaze darted between Elara and Lorien, suspicion and anger warring in his eyes. "You don't belong here, Elara. Beautiful songs don't change a thing! It's not safe. These... these creatures can't be trusted."

Elara flinched at his words, tears stinging her eyes. She looked to Lorien, silently begging for his support. The prince stepped forward, his hand still entwined with Elara's. "Sir, I assure you that Elara is safe here. No harm will come to her, I swear it."

Hector scoffed, his face reddening. "Your promises mean nothing to me. I've seen the destruction your kind can bring." He reached out, grasping Elara's wrist and pulling her towards him. "Come, Elara. We're leaving."

Elara stumbled, caught off guard by her father's rough grip. Lorien's hand tightened, anchoring her in place His gaze hardened as he turned to Hector, his voice low and commanding. "Release her." He stepped between them, his body a shield. "Never lay a hand on Elara in such a manner again. She is not a child to be dragged away against her will."

Hector's eyes widened, taken aback by Lorien's fierce protectiveness. He released Elara's wrist, his hand falling to his side. "She is my daughter," he growled, "and I will do what I must to keep her safe."

Elara's heart ached at the pain and fear in her father's voice. She stepped around Lorien, placing a gentle hand on Hector's arm. "Papa, please try to understand," she whispered, her eyes pleading. "I have found something precious here, something I never dreamed possible. Love, acceptance, a sense of belonging."

Hector's face crumpled, tears glistening in his eyes. "But what about us, Elara? Your family, your home? Are we not enough?"

Elara's heart broke at his words. "Of course you are, Papa. I love you and our village with all my heart. But I cannot deny the truth of what I feel here, the rightness of it."

She turned to Lorien, her eyes shining with unshed tears. "I don't know what the future holds," she admitted, "but I know that I cannot simply walk away from this, from you."

Lorien's expression softened, his hand coming up to cradle her cheek. "Elara, I would never ask you to choose between your world and mine. If your heart calls you back to your village, I will not stand in your way. But know that you will always have a place here, a home with me, if you wish it."

Hector's face hardened, his eyes darting between Elara and Lorien. "This is madness, Elara! You belong with your own kind, not with these creatures!"

The Queen stepped forward, her presence commanding attention. Her voice rang out, clear and authoritative. "I will not tolerate such disrespect in my realm."

She fixed Hector in a stern gaze. "Your daughter is a guest here, welcomed and cherished. She is under my protection, and I will not allow anyone, not even her own father, to dictate her choices or belittle her heart's desires."

Hector sputtered, his face reddening with indignation. "You have no right—"

"I have every right," the Queen interrupted, her voice sharp as a blade. "This is my kingdom and I have the last say. Human, faerie, it matters not. What matters is the content of one's heart, the purity of one's intentions."

She softened her tone, her eyes filled with compassion. "I understand your fear. The loss of a loved one is a tear that never really heals. But you must not let your grief and anger blind you to the beauty and possibility that still exists in this world."

Elara stepped forward, refusing to leave her father to his prejudice. "Papa, please. I know you blame the fairies for Mama's death, but it's not their fault. They are not the monsters you believe them to be."

Hector shook his head. "How can you say that, Elara? They took her from us. They lured her into the forest with their magic and she never came back."

Elara reached out and took her father's hand. "No, Papa. The fairies didn't lure Mama into the forest. I did." Her voice wavered, heavy with the weight of her confession. "I was the one who wandered into the forest that day, chasing a melody I heard on the wind. Mama followed me, trying to bring me back."

A single tear rolled down Hector's cheek as he listened. She continued, her voice etched with sadness. "It was an Orc that took Mama's life, not the fairies. They are not to blame for her death, and they are not to blame for my choices."

Elara's hazel eyes shimmered with tears as she looked up at her father, her voice barely above a whisper. "If you need someone to blame, Papa, blame me. I'm the reason Mama was in the forest that day. I'm the reason she's gone."

Hector's shoulders shook as he pulled Elara into a tight embrace, his tears falling freely. "No, it's not your fault. You were just a child, curious and full of wonder. I should have never let my grief turn into hatred. I should have never blamed the fairies for our loss."

He pulled back, cupping Elara's face in his hands. "Forgive me, Elara. Forgive me for my blindness, for my stubborn anger. I see now that I was wrong. The fairies are not our enemies. They are a part of this world, just as we are."

Elara smiled through her tears, her heart swelling with love and relief. "I forgive you, Papa. And I know Mama would forgive you too. She always said that love was the most powerful magic of all."

Hector nodded, a bittersweet smile on his lips. "She did, didn't she? I lost sight of that, but no more. I understand now, Elara. I understand why you need to stay, why your heart belongs here."

He glanced at Lorien and sighed. "I know I can't make you come home. Just promise me you'll be safe, that you'll always remember how much I love you."

Elara hugged her father tightly, whispering, "I promise, Papa. I'll always be your little girl, no matter where I am. And this parting isn't forever. I just need more time here, to understand," she looked back at Lorien, "who I am and what I want. This isn't goodbye, it's just a new beginning."

As they embraced, the lingering fairies and humans watched with misty eyes, each species trying to hide its emotion from the other.

Lorien stepped forward, placing a comforting hand on Elara's shoulder. His eyes met Hector's, a silent understanding passing between them. "Elara will always be welcome here, as will you and any of her human friends and family. All we ask is that you give notice and come with respect for our realm and our ways."

Hector nodded solemnly, his voice thick with emotion. "I understand. It'll take time for me to fully accept all of this, but I'll try. For Elara's sake and the memory of her mother, I'll try."

As the two men shook hands, a tentative truce forming, Cassia watched from the sidelines, her keen eyes observing the interaction. She couldn't help but catch the way Lorien looked at Elara, the way his touch seemed to linger just a moment longer than necessary.

"Elara, may I speak with you for a moment?" Cassia asked, her voice gentle yet insistent.

Elara nodded, wiping away the last of her tears as she followed Cassia just a few steps away, still not used to being able to walk away from Lorien. Cassia turned her back and spoke lowly so only Elara could hear. The redhead smiled and took Elara's hands in her own, her eyes reflecting both joy and concern.

"I've known you all your life... I'm not your ma, but I'm gonna be presumptive and speak for her with the question: What's going on between you and that Prince?"

Elara blushed. "I don't know, Cassia. It's all so new and confusing. I feel drawn to him in a way I can't explain."

Cassia smiled, squeezing Elara's hands reassuringly. "That's called love, my dear. And from what I've seen, it's not one-sided. He looks at you like you hung the stars in the sky."

"But what about the differences between our worlds? The barriers that separate us?"

"True love knows no boundaries," Cassia said sagely, her voice filled with conviction. "If your hearts are meant to be together, you'll find a way. Don't let fear hold you back from something beautiful. Besides, you've never been out of the village—but there have been known to be human and non-human couples. I have a friend who lives far and we write. She's married to a Fae."

Elara's mouth dropped.

"Not a royal one, mind you. But she says..." Cassia's voice dropped to a conspiratorial tone, "there are really no barriers when they are alone, if you know what I'm saying."

Elara yelped in surprise. Cassia had never spoken to her of such things.

"Oh child, grow up! If you haven't already, I'm sure you soon will. Just know, it's okay. Those that love you will love you no matter who you love, hear me?" Cassia wrapped her in a warm embrace and whispered, "I'm being presumptive again. This hug is from ya ma."

Elara nodded and let the tears fall. "You're right, Cassia. I can't let fear control me. I have to follow my heart wherever it may lead."

As the human villagers began their journey back home, Elara stood at the realm's edge, her heart heavy with the weight of her decision. She watched as the familiar faces of her friends and neighbors slowly disappeared into the distance, their backs turned to the enchanted world she had come to love. Her brother had given her a huge hug before he left, and promised to come back in a few days with some of her things. As he turned around now and gave her a wave, a big smile on his face, Elara already missed him.

The soft glow of the enchanted lights illuminated the villager's path before them, casting long shadows that seemed to dance with each step they took further away from her.

A gentle hand touched Elara's shoulder, and she turned to see Lorien standing beside her, his green eyes filled with understanding and compassion. In that moment, she knew that she had made the right choice. The love that had blossomed between them was a rare and precious thing, a bridge that could span the divide between their two worlds.

"I know it's not easy, watching everything you've ever known walk away," Lorien said. "But I promise you, Elara, I will be by your side every step of the way. You can leave whenever you want—"

"Leave?" Elara looked at him with worry in her eyes.

"Visit... visit whenever you want. You can spend as much time between our worlds as you want."

"But you have to stay here all the time."

"For now. You've been to the meetings. You know our current dilemma. But you Elara, are a ray of dapple sunlight through a canopy of war that looms. Of course, as you said when we first met, I'm selfish. I want you always by my side. But you're no prisoner."

Elara leaned into his touch, drawing strength from his presence. As the last of the villagers disappeared from view, Elara turned to face Lorien. "I'm scared," she admitted. "But I'm also hopeful. I believe that we can encourage an understanding that is possible between humans and fairies. Besides, they may not know about the Orc problem, but I have a terrible feeling that one day fairies and humans may need to come together to face a common problem. Better they learn to get along long before then."

Lorien smiled, his luminescent markings glowing with a soft, warm light. "You are a brave and remarkable woman, Elara. Together, we will show everyone that love knows no limits, that it can flourish in the most unexpected of places."

At the word "love" Elara felt like she could take flight without wings.

The two intertwined hands to head back to the castle when they passed the Queen, who was staring at the path the humans had disappeared down. Her thin fingers nested her chin, and she had a puzzled look on her face.

Elara paused, noticing the Queen's pensive expression. "Your Majesty, is everything alright?"

The Queen turned to Elara, her eyes clouded with confusion. "Elara, my dear, I couldn't help but replay your conversation with your father earlier. Something about your mother's death doesn't quite add up."

"What do you mean?"

"You see, Orcs are known for their brutality, but they also have a pattern. They never take their victims' bodies. They always leave them behind as a warning, a reminder of their savagery." A chill ran down Elara's spine as she processed the Queen's words. "But... we never found your mother's body."

"My father said the fairies must have taken it," Elara said. She realized how stupid that sounded now that she knew the fairies better.

The Queen shook her head, her golden hair catching the fading light. "No, Elara. We would never do such a thing. It goes against our very nature. If we found a human body, we would have given it back to the village."

Elara's mind raced, trying to make sense of this new information. Could it be possible that there was more to her mother's death than she had been led to believe? She glanced at Lorien, seeing the same questions reflected in his eyes.

"I don't understand," Elara whispered, her voice just audible above the rustling of the leaves.

The Queen placed a comforting hand on Elara's shoulder. "I don't know either. Not yet."

Something about the way the woman said it let Elara know that the Queen wasn't about to drop the puzzle of her mother's death.

Chapter 14

ELARA AND LORIEN STEPPED into the castle, their footsteps echoing through the grand hallway. Elara's hazel eyes sparkled excitedly as they locked onto Lorien's mesmerizing green gaze. The rhythm of their strides synchronized as if they moved to an unheard melody that only they could feel. Lorien's luminescent markings glowed in the dim light, casting a soft, warm light around them.

As they made their way down the corridor, Elara noticed a familiar figure waiting ahead. Aria stood still as a statue, her platinum hair cascading like a waterfall frozen in time. Her gaze, as cold as her blue eyes, was fixed on Elara.

Elara offered a reassuring smile that acknowledged the unspoken tension between them. She couldn't help but wonder what thoughts were racing through the woman's mind.

Despite the unease, Elara refused to let it dampen her spirits. She was determined to embrace this new chapter with open arms and heart. Leaning closer to Lorien, she whispered playfully, "I hope Aria doesn't plan on interrogating us. I've had enough of that for one lifetime."

Lorien chuckled, his voice like a gentle breeze carrying away her worries. "Fear not, my love. I'll protect you from any and all interrogations," he teased back, his eyes twinkling with mirth.

Aria stepped towards Elara, her movements as fluid as the wind itself. Her voice was calm and steady, yet there was an underlying current of tension that couldn't be ignored. "Elara, I know the spell is broken," she said, her words hanging in the air like a whispered secret. "But I don't understand why you didn't leave with the rest of the humans. What made you stay?"

Elara's heart skipped a beat at Aria's words. *How could she possibly know?* she wondered, her mind racing with possibilities. Before she could respond, Lorien interrupted, his voice filled with curiosity and a hint of skepticism.

"Aria, how could you possibly know that the spell is broken?" he asked, his brow furrowed in confusion. "We've only just discovered it ourselves."

Aria avoided Lorien's gaze, her eyes flickering to the floor as if seeking answers in the intricate patterns of the stone. "I figured out how to break the spell days ago."

Elara's eyes widened in surprise, a gasp escaping her lips. *Days ago?* She couldn't believe what she was hearing. Her mind raced with questions, trying to piece together the implications of Aria's revelation.

Lorien, too, seemed taken aback by Aria's confession. He took a step closer to her, his voice gentle yet probing. "Aria, why didn't you tell us sooner? We could have..." He trailed off, unsure of what to say.

Elara's heart ached for Aria, sensing the weight of the secret she had been carrying. She reached out, placing a comforting hand on Aria's arm. "I understand if you were hesitant to tell us. But please, help us understand. What made you keep this knowledge to yourself?"

The fae's ice-blue eyes finally met Elara's, a flicker of vulnerability shining through. "I... I was afraid. Afraid of what it might mean for all of us, for the kingdom, for... for Lorien."

Elara's heart went out to Aria, understanding the depth of her feelings for Lorien. She could tell that Aria was truly a good friend.

Aria took a deep breath, steadying herself as she prepared to share the truth she had kept hidden for so long. "The spell is about more than a mere understanding between the two bound parties. To be fulfilled, the bond must affect others around them, leading to acceptance and unity."

Lorien's brow furrowed as he listened, his mind grappling with the implications of Aria's words. "Acceptance and unity?" he echoed, his voice filled with a mix of curiosity and confusion. "What do you mean?"

Aria's gaze drifted to the intricate tapestries adorning the castle walls as if seeking guidance from the stories woven into their fabric. "The binding spell was never meant to be a mere contract between two individuals," she explained, her words carrying the weight of ancient wisdom. "It was designed to bridge the gap between our worlds, to foster understanding and harmony between fairies and humans."

Elara listened, and her eyes widened with realization as Aria's words sank in. Pieces of the puzzle began to fall into place in her mind, and a flicker of hope ignited within her heart. *The festival. The performance. The Queen's public words and actions... could they have triggered something in the hearts of those who witnessed them?*

As if reading her thoughts, Aria turned to Elara, a soft smile on her lips. "Your presence here, Elara, and the bond you share with Lorien... it has the power to inspire change, to shatter the barriers that have long divided our kinds."

Elara felt a surge of emotion rising within her, a mix of hope, happiness, and a newfound sense of purpose.

Lorien, too, seemed to be processing the weight of Aria's revelation. He reached out, taking Elara's hand in his own, his touch a reassuring anchor in the midst of the swirling emotions. "If what you say is true, Aria," he said, his voice filled with determination, "then we have a chance to make a real difference, to create a future where our kinds can coexist in harmony."

Aria nodded, a sad smile on her face.

Elara's mind raced, pieces of the puzzle clicking into place. *If Aria knew the spell could be broken, why didn't she say anything sooner?* A sudden realization dawned on her, and her heart sank. *Jealousy.* Aria's guarded demeanor and the subtle tension in her voice all made sense now.

Gathering her courage, Elara turned to Aria, her voice soft but determined. "Aria, may I speak with you privately for a moment?"

Aria's eyes widened slightly, but she nodded, her expression unreadable. Lorien gave Elara's hand a gentle squeeze before stepping away, allowing the two women their space.

Elara took a deep breath. "Aria, when I first arrived here, I was filled with hate and anger. The last thing I expected was to fall in love." Her voice shook, but she pressed on. "I know I wasn't entirely honest with you earlier, and for that, I apologize. But things have changed."

Aria remained silent, her posture stiff, but her eyes seemed to smile, a flicker of understanding passing between them. Elara continued, her words tumbling out in a rush of emotion. "I never meant to hurt you or to come between you and Lorien. But what we have... it's real, and it's powerful. I know you care for him, and I can't imagine how difficult this must be for you."

A single tear rolled down Aria's cheek, but she quickly brushed it away. "I've known Lorien my entire life, and I've loved him for as long as I can remember. Seeing him with you... it's not easy."

Elara's heart ached for Aria, and she reached out, tentatively placing a hand on the fairy's arm. "I'm so sorry, Aria. I never wanted to cause you pain. But I also can't deny what I feel for Lorien. Is there any way we can find a path forward together?"

Aria took a deep breath, her gaze flickering between Elara and Lorien's distant figure . "I didn't tell you how to break the spell because I could see from the beginning that your bond with Lorien was about more than just magic." Her voice wavered, but she pressed on. "I was afraid that if others accepted you as bonded, I'd lose any chance I had with him."

Elara's heart felt heavy with the weight of Aria's confession. The fairy's voice grew quieter, tinged with resignation. "But the truth is,

Lorien has known me our whole lives, and he's never looked at me the way he looks at you."

A moment of silence stretched between them, the air thick with unspoken emotions. Finally, Aria straightened her shoulders, a determined glint in her eyes. "I won't interfere, Elara. I promise to leave you and Lorien alone to explore this connection without any obstacles from me."

Elara's eyes widened in surprise, and before she could think twice, she stepped forward and embraced Aria in a tight hug. She stiffened for a moment, then slowly relaxed into the embrace. Elara's voice was soft but filled with sincerity. "Thank you, Aria. But I don't want you to leave us alone."

Aria pulled back, confusion etched on her face. Elara offered a warm smile. "I'm new to this kingdom, and I'm going to need friends. I was hoping that you might be my first one here."

A flicker of surprise danced in Aria's eyes, followed by a tentative smile. "You want me to be your friend? Even after everything?"

Elara nodded, her smile growing wider. "Especially after everything. We may have gotten off to a rocky start, but I believe we have more in common than we realize. And I would be honored to call you my friend, Aria."

The fairy's smile blossomed into a genuine grin, and she reached out to squeeze Elara's hand. "I think I'd like that, Elara. A fresh start, as friends."

Lorien, sensing the shift in the atmosphere, approached the two women, his curiosity piqued. His piercing green eyes darted between Elara and Aria, a hint of amusement tugging at the corners of his lips. "And what, pray tell, has brought about this sudden camaraderie?" he asked, his voice rich with genuine interest.

Elara turned to face him, her vibrant hazel eyes sparkling with mirth. A soft chuckle escaped her lips, light and infectious, as she playfully swatted at Lorien's arm. "It's girl talk, and you'd do well to mind your own business, Your Highness."

Lorien's laughter echoed through the hallway, warm and melodic. He raised an eyebrow, a teasing glint in his eyes. "Is that so? And here I thought I might finally witness you addressing me with the proper respect my title deserves."

Elara's grin widened, and she stepped closer to Lorien, her voice lowering to a conspiratorial whisper. "Well, if you insist on the formalities, I suppose I can manage a curtsy and a demure 'Your Highness' in public. But in private, or among friends..." She winked, her tone turning playful. "You'll just have to accept me as I am, title or no."

Aria, watching the exchange, couldn't help but laugh, the sound like the tinkling of wind chimes. She shook her head, her platinum hair shimmering in the soft light. "You two are quite the pair. I must admit, I'm looking forward to getting to know the human who has managed to capture the heart of our esteemed Prince."

Lorien's gaze softened as he looked at Elara, a tender expression on his face. "She's one of a kind, Aria. I have no doubt you'll come to see that as well."

Elara felt a warmth bloom in her chest at Lorien's words. She marveled at the turn of events, at the unexpected friendship blossoming with Aria and the deepening connection with Lorien. At this moment, surrounded by the magic of the faerie realm and the promise of new beginnings, Elara felt a sense of belonging, a glimmer of hope for the future that stretched out before them.

As Aria bid them farewell and disappeared down the hallway, Elara turned to Lorien, her heart fluttering with anticipation.

As they entered their room, a sense of newfound freedom washed over them as they took in the familiar surroundings with a fresh perspective. The absence of the binding spell's restrictions made the space feel different as if the very air itself had changed. They exchanged glances, a mixture of excitement and uncertainty dancing in their eyes.

Elara, still shy despite their shared experiences, made her way behind the privacy curtain to change for the night. As she slipped into a beautiful, flowing sleeping gown, she couldn't help but marvel at how the delicate fabric felt against her skin, as if it were woven from the essence of magic itself. She doubted she'd ever get used to the fabrics and exquisite tailoring of the fairies.

When she emerged from behind the curtain, Lorien's breath caught in his throat. He had lit enchanted candles that hovered in space, giving off warm amber light. The soft light seemed to embrace Elara, highlighting her natural beauty. Her warm, hazel eyes sparkled with a mixture of surprise and delight as she noticed Lorien's awestruck expression.

Lorien, his heart pounding in his chest, reached into his pocket, his fingers closing around a small, delicate piece of enchanted jewelry. He had been waiting for the perfect moment to present this gift to Elara. He pulled the jewelry out with a gentle tug, holding it up for Elara to see.

"Elara, I want you to have this. It's a token of my affection, a reminder of the magic we share."

Elara's eyes widened as she took in the exquisite craftsmanship of the enchanted jewelry. With trembling fingers, she reached out to take the gift, her heart swelling with gratitude and love. She could feel the magical energy coursing through it.

"Lorien, it's beautiful," she whispered, her voice thick with emotion. "I don't know what to say. "

As she held the jewelry in her hands, Elara looked up at Lorien, her eyes shining with unshed tears. "Thank you, Lorien. Not just for this but for everything. For seeing me, for accepting me, for loving me."

Lorien reached out and gently stroked Elara's cheek with his thumb. "You've changed my world, Elara. You've shown me the true meaning of love, of connection. I am the one who should be thanking you."

As Elara fastened the jewelry around her neck, she could feel the magic of their love thrumming through her very being.

Lorien's eyes sparkled with mischief as he leaned in close, his breath tickling Elara's ear. "You know, there is a way you could show me your gratitude."

Elara's heart skipped a beat, her skin tingling with anticipation. She met Lorien's gaze, her eyes dancing with a playful light. "Oh? And what might that be, my prince?"

With a flick of his fingers, Lorien summoned his magic, and the two beds in the room began to move, sliding together until they formed a single, expansive space. The room around them seemed to fade into the background, the soft glow of enchanted candles casting a warm, inviting light.

Elara's breath caught in her throat as Lorien's arms encircled her waist, drawing her close. Their bodies moved in perfect harmony as if they were meant to be together. The passion that had been simmering between them finally found its release, and they came together in a sensual, intimate kiss.

Lorien's hands roamed Elara's body, tracing the smooth curves and sharp angles with reverent fascination. Every touch sent a jolt of electricity through her, igniting a fire that burned deep within her core. Elara reciprocated, her hands moving with delicate precision as they explored the luminescent markings that adorned Lorien's skin. The patterns seemed to come alive under her touch, pulsing and glowing like miniature stars. Lorien's lips moved down her neck, sucking gently on her skin. His tongue flicked against her earlobe, sending shivers down her spine. Elara's soft moans filled the room, echoing off the walls.

Elara arched her back, pressing her body closer to Lorien's. She felt his hardness against her and knew she was ready for him. As she slipped out of her gown and wrapped her legs around his waist, he whispered, "Why'd you even put it on?"

As their bodies moved together in a rhythm only they shared, their kisses deepened, their tongues dancing and twirling in a sensual dance. Her hands slid down his chest, feeling the softness of his skin. Elara gasped as she felt Lorien's hardness pressing against her, a clear indication of his desire. She ground her hips forward, wanting more of that heat.

Lorien's wings, usually hidden from view, unfurled in a shimmering display of iridescent beauty. She touched the wings that now seemed to pulse with life, feeling the soft feathers beneath her fingertips. They were smooth, like the finest silk, and Elara couldn't resist running her fingers along their delicate edges. She remembered how he told her to stroke them before and allowed her hands to dance across his wings, varying the pressure. She moved toward the top of the wing and could tell it was more sensitive. Lorien gasped, a shudder of pleasure rippling through him at her touch.

"You're so beautiful," he whispered, trailing kisses down her jawline as he spoke. His hand found the sensitive spots along Elara's spine, drawing out soft moans of ecstasy as he caressed her. His other hand slid up her stomach and cupped one exposed breast, squeezing gently before rolling a nipple between his fingers. A soft moan escaped Elara's lips as she arched into him. He smirked, enjoying her reaction. She reached back with one hand to caress his wings again while the other hand roamed lower down his body, tracing the muscles in his back before cupping his ass cheek and pulling him closer as she ground herself against him once more.

At that moment, all the barriers between them fell away. They were no longer fae and human, prince and commoner. They were simply two souls, bound by love and magic, discovering the depths of their connection in the most intimate way possible.

Lorien's breath quickened as Elara's touch ignited sparks along his skin. His hands explored the curves of her body reverently, as if memorizing every dip and swell.

Elara gasped as Lorien's fingers found the apex of her thighs, stroking and teasing. Magical energy hummed between them, heightening every sensation. She could feel the thrum of his heartbeat as she pressed closer, skin against skin. Reaching between them, she took his hardened length in hand, relishing the silken heat against her palm.

Lorien groaned, his voice rough with desire. He positioned himself at her entrance and with a smooth thrust, joined their bodies as one. They moved together in perfect synchronicity, like partners in an ancient dance. Elara cried out in bliss as he filled and stretched her, hitting a sweet spot deep inside.

Their lovemaking was as natural as breathing, an instinctual rhythm pulsing between them. Hands grasped, and mouths explored as they climbed the peak of ecstasy together. Magic crackled in the air, responding to the intensity of their bond.

"I love you with everything I am," Elara panted against Lorien's ear.

"And I you, my heart," he returned fervently, punctuating his words with a deep thrust that had her seeing stars.

Their movements grew more fevered, chasing the ultimate pleasure. When it crested over them, they clung to each other, bodies shaking, souls merging as they rode out the waves of rapture.

As they drifted down from the high, limbs deliciously heavy, Lorien gathered Elara close. He brushed damp hair strands from her face, his touch achingly tender. Jade eyes met hazel ones, brimming with love and contentment. No words were needed in the afterglow—only the mingling of their breaths and the synchronous beating of their hearts, two halves of a whole.

Chapter 15

THE MORNING SUN DAPPLED through the shimmering leaves of the castle's gardens. Elara strolled alongside Lorien, her face unable to hide her bliss and contentment.

"So, what's on the agenda for today?" Elara asked, hurrying to follow Lorien's graceful strides. She couldn't help but marvel at how the light caught the luminescent patterns on his skin, painting him in an ethereal radiance. She also couldn't help but remember the was they pulsed when the two of them reached certain peaks the night prior.

Lorien tilted his head, his silver hair cascading like a waterfall over his shoulder. "I have some duties to attend to in the heart of the forest." His green eyes met hers, a hint of mischief dancing within their depths. "And you? Any grand adventures planned?"

Elara laughed. "Oh, you know me. I thought I might explore more of the castle, maybe even try my hand at some faerie melodies." She tapped out a playful rhythm on the nearby railing, her fingers moving with an innate musicality.

Lorien's gaze softened, a warmth spreading through his chest at the sight of Elara so at ease in his world. "I have no doubt you'll charm everyone within earshot," he teased, his voice laced with affection.

As they reached a fork in the path, Elara felt a flutter of reluctance to part ways. Even though the binding spell no longer tethered them together, she found herself gravitating towards Lorien, drawn by an inexplicable pull. She hesitated, her hand lingering on his arm.

"I'll see you later." It was more a question than a statement, hinting at a promise whispered between kindred spirits.

Lorien nodded, his reluctance mirrored in the gentle brush of his fingers against hers. "Always."

With a final shared smile, they went their separate ways, yet the connection between them remained unbroken, like a shimmering thread that defied distance and magic alike.

As Elara wandered through the castle's halls, her thoughts drifted to Lorien, to the way his presence filled her with a sense of belonging she had never known before. She hummed a soft melody, the notes weaving together like the strands of their intertwined destinies.

✕

IN THE DEPTHS OF THE forest, Lorien found his own thoughts turning to Elara, to the way her laughter seemed to make the very air sparkle with joy. He moved through his duties with a newfound lightness in his step, the weight of centuries of solitude lifting with each passing moment spent in her company.

Lorien's presence must have seemed far away because Taliesin, who walked next to him, gave a playful bump. "So, Lorien, I never thought I'd see the day when you'd fall for a human," Taliesin teased, his eyes dancing with amusement. "Quite the rebellious streak you've developed." His friend's ever-mischievous grin never faltered.

Lorien shook his head, a smile tugging at the corners of his lips. "I haven't broken any laws, Taliesin. Elara and I... it's different."

"Oh, I know," Taliesin laughed. "You've only broken social norms and the hearts of countless fae maidens in the process."

Lorien chuckled, the sound echoing through the ancient trees. "As much as I enjoy your teasing, we must focus on the council meeting. A scout has returned with information about the Orcs' movements."

Taliesin's expression sobered, his playful demeanor giving way to the sharp intellect that lay beneath. "Of course." But two steps before entering the council, never turning to look at his friend or losing stride, Taliesin added "I forgot to ask? Does she have a sister? Asking for a friend."

Lorien's steps faltered, and then he shook his head and followed Taliesin. His friend never really could be serious for very long.

As they entered the council chamber, Lorien's thoughts lingered on Elara. Even amidst of duty and responsibility, she was never far from his mind.

✕

MEANWHILE, ELARA FOUND herself in the company of Aria, who had offered to show her around the kingdom. As they walked, Elara marveled at the sprawling expanse of the realm, realizing that what she had seen so far was merely a fraction of its true size.

"It's incredible," Elara breathed, her eyes wide with wonder. "I had no idea the kingdom was so vast."

Aria smiled, a hint of pride in her voice. "It is truly a sight to behold. There are so many hidden wonders waiting to be discovered."

As they explored, Elara couldn't help but perceived slight tension in Aria's demeanor. She wondered if it had something to do with her growing closeness to Lorien, but she pushed the thought aside, determined to forge a friendship with the fae maiden.

"Thank you for showing me around, Aria," Elara said sincerely. "It means a lot to me."

"You're welcome, Elara. I know it can't be easy, being so far from home."

As they continued their tour, Elara felt a growing sense of belonging, a budding connection to the realm and its inhabitants. She couldn't wait to share her discoveries with Lorien. He'd probably laugh. Every day she told him of something new she'd 'found' and he would just listen, amusement written on his lips. Of course, it was no discovery to him.

Elara's ears picked up on a conversation nearby as they walked through a particularly enchanting garden. Two fairies, voices hushed but not quite low enough to escape notice, were discussing her presence in the kingdom.

"I don't know what to make of it," one faerie said, her tone skeptical. "A human, living among us? It's unheard of."

The other nodded, a frown creasing her delicate features. "I worry about the consequences. What if it upsets the balance of ... *things*?"

Elara felt a knot form in her stomach, their words stinging like nettles. She had been so caught up in the wonder of the realm that she hadn't stopped to consider how others might perceive her presence.

Aria, noticing Elara's unease, placed a comforting hand on her shoulder. "Don't let their words trouble you," she said softly. "There are plenty of fairies who are happy to have you here. Change is never easy, but it is often necessary for growth."

Elara managed a grateful smile, but the doubts lingered, a shadow on her heart.

LATER THAT DAY, AS the sun began to dip towards the horizon, Elara found herself once again walking with Lorien through the castle gardens. While the pair often found they had the gardens to themselves during morning strolls, several other couples were walking hand-in-hand in the evening. There were also a few families. Oakley's son had found them almost as soon as they entered the garden. He did his trick of growing a flower in his hand to that matched Elara's dress and gave it to her with a broad smile. It had become an exchange that happened every time he saw her, sometimes several times a day. Elara loved it.

"Are you trying to court the same woman as your prince?" Lorien asked sternly, but there was amusement on his face.

The boy just shrugged. "Well, my 'ma says variety is always best. I'm giving her choices."

The boy darted off toward his father before a shocked Lorien could respond. Elara burst out laughing.

"I like that. Choices. I have choices."

Lorien just shot her an annoyed look. "That kid is rude."

"Yes, but cute."

As they continued walking, a figure emerged from the shadows, her presence commanding and regal. It was the Queen flanked by two attendants. It was surprising, as she rarely took evening strolls in the garden.

"Elara, Lorien," she greeted them, her voice a soothing melody. She walked over and placed an arm around Elara. "How have you been treated?"

"Very well," Elara said. She gushed about the 'discoveries' she made with Aria earlier. She didn't mention the conversations she'd overheard. The Queen just allowed her to talk, the same look on her face as her son, both attempting to restrain a chuckle.

"I'm glad you're enjoying yourself and finding new things. And I am especially elated about how you've made my son happy. It's good for the people to see a happy prince falling in love with such a wonderful young woman."

Elara felt her cheeks warm.

"Your love has the power to bridge the gap between our worlds," the Queen continued, her gaze settling on Elara. "But I know that the path ahead will not be easy. There will be those who doubt, who fear the change you represent."

She reached out, taking the couple's joined hands in her own. A soft glow emanated from her touch, a warmth that spread through Elara's being.

"I offer you my blessing," the Queen said, her voice resonating with ancient power. "May your love be a light in the darkness, a beacon of hope for all who seek to find common ground."

Elara felt tears prick at the corners of her eyes, overwhelmed by the Queen's acceptance and support. Lorien, too, seemed moved, his eyes shining with gratitude.

"Thank you, Mother. Your blessing means more than you know."

The Queen smiled with a radiant warmth that seemed to illuminate the garden. "You have my support son, always. Together, you can change hearts and minds and forge a new path forward."

As the Queen took her leave, Elara looked after her in wonder.

"Your mother is amazing."

Lorien laughed. "She would not disagree."

Elara looked down at her palms. They were warm, and there was a faint glow in the center. She looked up at Lorien.

"Think of it like an animal scenting its area," he said. When Elara made a face of confused disgust, he added, "Anyone who is magically attuned will know you have a connection with whoever gave the blessing. And anyone around here would recognize that magical marking as my mother's."

Elara's eyes widened, realizing that no small thing had just happened.

"Hey, why haven't you marked me?"

He raised his eyebrows. "I did. Last night, don't you remember?"

He walked off, leaving Elara standing, mouth agape. She caught up a few paces later and punched him lightly on the arm.

"Still no respect for my title?" He chuckled, taking her hand in his.

As they walked through the garden, Elara couldn't help but notice the reactions of the fairies they passed. Some smiled warmly, inclining their heads in respectful acknowledgment. Others seemed surprised, their eyes widening as they took in the sight of the human and fae prince together. But none openly expressed discontent or disapproval.

Elara leaned closer to Lorien, whispering, "Do you think they know about your mother's blessing?"

Lorien squeezed her hand reassuringly. "Word travels fast in the faerie realm. And even if they didn't know, I told you, they can pick up on it."

A sense of relief washed over Elara. The Queen's public display of support had set the stage for a more harmonious coexistence between humans and fairies. It also seemed that it would mean that even fairies not too fond of her presence would respectfully hold their tongues. She felt a newfound sense of ease knowing that she had the blessing of the royal family.

A familiar figure caught Elara's eye as they approached the castle gates. Her heart leaped with joy as she recognized her brother, Dante, waiting for them with a wide grin on his face.

"Dante!" Elara exclaimed, releasing Lorien's hand and running to embrace her brother.

Dante laughed, lifting Elara off her feet and spinning her around. "I told you I'd come visit, didn't I?"

Lorien approached them, a warm smile on his face. "Welcome, Dante. It's good to see you again."

Dante set Elara down and extended his hand to Lorien. "Likewise, Your Highness. I come bearing gifts for my sister."

He gestured to a satchel slung over his shoulder. Elara's eyes lit up with curiosity. "What did you bring?"

"Just a few things from home to make you feel more comfortable here," Dante replied, handing her the bag.

As Elara rummaged through the contents, her eyes brimming with tears of gratitude, Dante turned to Lorien. "I want you to know that you have my full support. I've never seen Elara happier than when she's with you."

Lorien placed a hand on Dante's shoulder, his expression sincere. "Thank you, Dante. Your acceptance means the world to us, but especially to her."

Elara looked up from the pouch and began jumping up and down like an excited child. "You brought my instruments!"

Dante smiled and pushed his hands into his pockets. "And bread from the village. I'm sure the food here is amazing, but you loved that bread. No clothes though." He looked from his sister to Lorien. "You look better in the clothes from here. Your Highness, you met her wearing the frumpy old dress she wears when doing chores? And *that* caught your eye?"

Elara rolled her eyes and Lorien laughed and shrugged.

"Why don't you stay and eat with us? And stay the night?" Lorien asked. He waved at some attendants to give instructions. "It's late."

Dante grinned. "That would be great! Thank you!" He turned to Elara. "We should spend some time together. I won't be around for a bit."

Elara looked confused. Dante pulled out a crumpled piece of paper from his pocket. She looked over it, and her eyes widened.

"Conscripted to the king's army?"

Dante shrugged. "I'm not the only one. No one really knows why, but it doesn't matter. The king calls, and you go."

Elara's brows knitted together with concern. "But why now? The kingdom has been at peace for years."

Lorien exchanged a glance with Dante before speaking. "There have been rumors of Orc movements in the borderlands. Our scouts have reported increased activity."

Elara's heart skipped a beat. The memory of her mother's disappearance and the face of the Orc emerging from the trees rushed back to her. She took a steadying breath, pushing the thoughts aside.

"Let's not dwell on this now," Dante said, sensing his sister's unease. "I'm here to celebrate with you."

As if on cue, the sound of music drifted through the air. Fairies and humans alike were gathering in the courtyard, the atmosphere alive with excitement. A few humans from the village had been visiting every day—usually the same ones. It appears some of them were making friends among the fairies. It was heartwarming to see.

Dante shrugged. "I didn't come with them. They were already here."

"We know. There are a few every evening." Lorien offered his arm to Elara. "Shall we?"

She smiled, taking his arm as they walked towards the group, Dante following close behind.

The courtyard was a sight to behold. Lights twinkled in the trees, casting a warm glow over the scene. Humans and fairies mingled freely, laughter and chatter filling the air. Elara couldn't help but notice that most of those around her were younger.

Elara marveled at the sight. At this moment, the barriers between their worlds seemed to melt away. Love, in all its forms, was the common thread that bound them together.

As they joined the celebration, Elara couldn't help but reflect on the journey that had brought her here. The pain of her past and the uncertainty of her future seemed to fade amid the twinkling lights.

The celebration continued late into the night, word spreading that the Prince had made special arrangements for them to stay longer since Dante was visiting at the same time.

Lorien led Elara to the center of the courtyard, where couples were dancing to the enchanting music played by a group of musicians. As they began to sway to the melody, Lorien pulled her close, his eyes locking with hers.

No words needed to be said. They danced, lost in each other's embrace.

Nearby, Dante conversed with a group of curious fairies, eager to learn more about human life. He regaled them with tales of his adventures, though he was embellishing just a bit.

"You know, I never thought I'd find myself so engrossed in the stories of a human," one of the fairies remarked. "I thought your short lives were chores, chores, and more chores."

Dante grinned, raising his glass as if in a toast. "Here is to chores! It's a lot of that, but so much more. And you, my friends, have shown me that there's so much more to the realm than I ever imagined. Here's to a future of new friendships and adventures!"

As the night wore on, the atmosphere grew even more festive. Laughter rang out as fairies and humans alike shared tales and jokes, their differences forgotten in the spirit of camaraderie.

Elara and Lorien, still wrapped in each other's arms, watched the scene with a sense of pride and hope. They knew their love had sparked something greater, a movement towards unity that would shape the future of both their realms.

And though neither would say it, both were thinking that sooner rather than later both sides would be happy to have friends who could become allies.

As the first light of dawn began to paint the sky, casting a golden glow over the courtyard, both knew this was just the beginning. A new chapter was unfolding. While not yet written, each was happy to have the other in their story, to face the dark days ahead together.

Let's stay in touch!

Sign up for my newsletter for book announcements, a bit of Morgan, and of course some freebies and giveaways.

Don't miss out!

Visit the website below and you can sign up to receive emails whenever Morgan Sterling publishes a new book. There's no charge and no obligation.

https://books2read.com/r/B-A-YOGEB-BWYDF

BOOKS 2 READ

Connecting independent readers to independent writers.

Did you love *Golden Melodies*? Then you should read *Stellar Harmony* by Morgan Sterling!

Stellar Harmony
An urban romance written in the stars
By Morgan Sterling
A Nerdy Love Affair Book 1

Prepare for a journey where the stars align in unexpected ways. Meet Langston, an academic prodigy straddling two worlds: the rigorous confines of academia and the vibrant pulse of his urban roots. Opposite him stands Aurora, a heartbroken R&B songstress seeking solace amidst the melodies of her past. When their paths converge at an open mic night, their connection ignites with a force that defies logic.

As Langston grapples with the pressures of his academic pursuits and the pull of his community, Aurora battles to reclaim her voice in an industry tainted by betrayal. Together, they navigate the complexities of love, trust, and self-discovery against a backdrop of starry nights and whispered promises.

But as their bond deepens, they must confront the shadows of their pasts. Langston's insecurities threaten to eclipse their budding romance, while Aurora's struggle for artistic freedom jeopardizes everything she holds dear. Can they find harmony amidst the chaos of their lives, or will their love be lost among the stars?

Join Langston and Aurora on a cosmic odyssey where passion collides with purpose, and the universe itself becomes a stage for their *Stellar Harmony*.

Also by Morgan Sterling

A Nerdy Love Affair
Stellar Harmony

Braided Realms
Golden Melodies

Milton Keynes UK
Ingram Content Group UK Ltd.
UKHW030949261124
451585UK00001B/110